A Woman Walked into the Bar

(Stories)

Linda H. Heuring

All Nations Press
P.O. Box 10821, Tallahassee, FL 32302

Someone must be blamed for what you see here. I blame my mother who started all this by teaching me to read before I was old enough for school. My grandparents for providing me a forum to create and perform these stories live on front porches and in family rooms. My dad for knowing this is exactly what I should do with my life and reading and reading and reading everything I ever wrote. You can blame my amazing editors Donna J. Long and Rick Campbell of All Nations Press for choosing this collection, and Nancy, Jan, Alison, and Tania, who took time from their own work to read and give feedback. Blame Velicia, who turned an idea into a work of art. Blame Clem and the editors at Fish who thought my work worthy of an Irish audience, and Roderick at *Rosebud* who had the uncanny ability to choose another story just as discouragement started to set in. Blame the Fury's Ferry Writers and Louise who taught me to "put it in a story." Most importantly, blame Whatley and his WWoWWWoWSW.

—LHH

Copyright © 2017 by Linda H. Heuring

Cover design: Velicia Jerus Darquenne
Front cover photograph: Linda H. Heuring

ISBN: 978-0-9912721-3-6
Printed in the USA on acid-free paper

Praise for *A Woman Walked into the Bar*

In this amazing debut collection, Heuring deepens our understanding of the shapes of grief, passion, and sacrifice, effortlessly revealing how we connect, how we depend on one another, how our lives are intertwined beyond the cultures that have defined us.

—Nancy Takacs, 2016 poetry winner
of the Juniper Prize for *The Worrier*

Linda H. Heuring's engaging and deftly written short stories are warm invitations to homes in our shared American community. Her characters welcome the reader with the kindness of neighbors, their stories beckoning by an intriguing combination of mystery and motivation, like the best secrets in town. Whether the characters live in Kentucky country or Florida seaside, they are linked to each other and to the reader by their shared humanity. Heuring imbues characters in conflict with both empathy and exactitude, as shown in "Three of Them," as a wife learns to empathize with her fading father-in-law, and in "Chaperone for Cousin Katie," as a student covers for her idealized cousin on the eve of her elopement. Whether family or friendship ties, Heuring's kind but sharp eye is complemented by her humor. For even from the shell of a half-burnt home in "Bordering on Sainthood," Heuring's dialogue crackles like the fire that destroyed the house. In this collection of beautifully crafted stories, readers will not only understand the characters of *A Woman Walked into the Bar*, but care about them like neighbors of their own.

—Alison Ruth, author of *Near-Mint Cinderella*
and *Starlight Black and the Misfortune Society*

ACKNOWLEDGEMENTS

The author wishes to acknowledge and thank the publications where these stories first appeared, as well as the judges who chose or nominated stories for the following awards:

"Little Mister," *Crack the Spine*, Issue 165; reprinted in *Crack the Spine Anthology XIV* (2016); (Second Place, as "Mr. Fisher's Value Lesson," Union County Writer's Club).

"Breaking Point," *The Broad River Review*, 2015 (finalist for the Rash Award in Fiction, 2014).

"Until There's Not," *Crannog* (Ireland), October 2015

"A Woman Walked into the Bar"; shortlisted for the 2014 Bridport Prize, United Kingdom.

"Nibbling at the Bloodstains," *Alabama Literary Review*, 2013

"Three of Them," *Clover, A Literary Rag*, December 2013

"Whatever Will Do," *Clover, A Literary Rag*, summer 2013 (Third Place, E.S. Smith Short Story Prize, 2011; judge Daniel Handler; longlisted for the Fish Short Story Prize).

"Side of Bacon," *The Southern Women's Review*, 2012 (First Place 2009 Fiction Competition, Union County Writers Club, and nominated for Best of the Net).

"One Chair Away," *Concho River Review*, fall 2012 (First Place 2011 Fiction Competition, Union County Writers Club).

"Bordering on Sainthood," *Kestrel*, fall 2012 (nominated for the Pushcart Prize).

"Roommates," *Fish Anthology*, July 2012 (winner of the Fish International Short Story Prize, Ireland, 2011; judge David Mitchell).

"Victim of Circumstance," *Rosebud*, fall 2010

"Chaperone for Cousin Katie," *Rosebud*, spring 2008

To Shirley
because she asked
and to David
because he didn't.

Table of Contents

ON CURSED GROUND

They don't talk to her here, but they know who she is. They cross themselves. Pretend to brush lint. Today the post office clerk touched a necklace. *Likely a totem*, Tina thought.

Tina's mail had piled up in three weeks. Two totebags full. She shoved one onto the floor of her pickup and reached for the other. A rusty-eyed maltese in a pink rhinestone collar pranced up to her. Tina reached out to pet her, but the dog skittered backward, dragged by a retracted leash attached to a turbaned woman in a flowered shift. The woman snatched up the dog, racked her neck back like a rooster, narrowed her eyes, and spat on the sidewalk at Tina's feet. Three times. Phlegm sizzled on concrete.

Acid rose in Tina's throat. Spitting. That was a new one. She tossed the second bag on the passenger seat, drove straight home, and crawled into bed.

She woke thirsty with a growling stomach. It was just light or almost dark, she couldn't tell which. Her watch said six. She carried a glass of water onto the screen porch. The sun was in the east. She had slept through until morning.

The air was light with promise, but Tina was weighed down. A chain of deaths had wrapped around her, steel links forged so close together they didn't have time to rust in the humidity before the next one was hammered on. She carried the load with every step. She crossed the black dirt of her yard and stood on her listing dock at the water's edge. The cypress on the opposite shore formed a right angle with its reflection, a taunting bridge to nowhere but the soft mud below the surface. She saw herself sinking, the last bubbles of air from her lungs dancing toward the flat surface of the bayou, her body anchored to the bottom with a concrete block.

"No," she said aloud in the silent swamp. A concrete block was too much, too predictable. Too mafiaesque. An old tractor tire? Seriously, here? Maybe a boat battery. She looked behind her and saw the perfect weight: an outboard motor, the one that threw a rod last year, its upside-down metal cover just another mosquito incubator. Jason was going to fix it. Someday. One day. Or use it for parts. Too good to throw away and yet no use to anyone the way it was. The correlation was not lost on her.

Tires crunched on the shell road, and the cherry-red paint of a Ford Ranger flashed through the trees. Only Mary Jo Mobley could take the turn-off at that speed. Checking on her, no doubt. Mary Jo was the one friend who hadn't turned her back, even when Tina had turned off her phone and thrown weeks of mail, unopened, in a milk crate on the porch.

At first people brought food, sent cards. But as the deaths piled up, seven for those who were counting, and Tina certainly was, the sympathetic hugs disappeared, replaced by a circle of fear. What curse had picked off all the men in her family over the last eleven months? Done in one-by-one except for the two uncles lost in a single boating accident. Snuffed out. Eliminated. A heart attack. An embolism. A spider bite. A stroke. And finally her husband Jason, whose shoulder she'd leaned on through all the others, his pickup buried by a load of pine from a passing log truck.

"Glad to see you out of bed," Mary Jo said. "I brought beignets. Still warm."

"Is that why you threw half my gravel into the swamp coming in?"

"No, that was just for fun."

Mary Jo unpacked her care package: a pound can of Cafe du Monde, a sweating bottle of half and half, and a dozen eggs. Tina ripped a paper towel from the roll on the kitchen table and chose a pastry from the box. A puff of powdered sugar fell onto the table. Mary Jo started the coffee.

"Eggs? One of my clients brought them by this morning," Mary Jo said. She held up a cast iron skillet.

"Does anybody pay you in dollars?" Tina said.

Mary Jo frowned and cracked an egg against the side of the skillet. The yellow broke. "For that, you get a broken one," she said.

"I'm just saying," Tina said.

"Hey, it's my business model. Eggs today. Tomorrow? Tomatoes."

"Or a chicken," Tina said. She tackled another beignet. Mary Jo slapped the egg on a plate and tackled the kitchen counter with a soapy sponge.

"At least I'm seeing clients. You seem to have alienated all of yours." Mary Jo scrubbed at a caked-on clump on the formica. "What the hell is this? It's like cement."

"Beans. Rice. Beans and rice. I didn't ask you to clean it."

"What are you being so shitty with me for? I came bearing gifts."

"And criticism."

"You started it with the egg crack."

"Chalk it up to one of the five stages of grief. Take your pick. I'm in all of them simultaneously." Tina pushed past Mary Jo to put her plate in the sink.

Mary Jo closed her eyes and took in a deep breath. She had taught Tina to center herself like that, a kind of a spiritual reset button when things got off track. Tina was so far off the track she didn't even bother anymore. Mary Jo was a healer. She'd be a shaman in another era, and maybe she had been. Whatever you believed, she was the only human stubborn enough to venture out here and be abused.

Tina touched her on the shoulder. Mary Jo stiffened and opened her eyes.

"I'm sorry," Tina said. She took a deep breath. "Hi, Mary Jo. Thanks for the breakfast."

"Your energy is a mess," Mary Jo said.

"No shit."

Things weren't such a mess on the porch. They sat in rocking chairs and faced the water.

"I dreamed about you last night," Mary Jo said.

This was the real reason for today's visit, Tina realized. She rocked slowly, waiting.

"You were underwater . . ."

Tina shivered. It wasn't that she would really take that plunge. She was just so . . . She didn't know what she was. Numb?

"How do you do it, Mary Jo? There's no CCTV out here. Swamp cam? I know, swami cam."

"We don't all wear purple and see fairies dancing in the wind. You and I are connected. What can I say?" She sipped coffee. "So, tell me, Tina, that I don't have to worry about dragging the swamp with a grappling hook."

"God, Mary Jo. Paint me a picture, why don't you."

"I don't have to paint. Just look at your own stuff. I'm sure there's one or two on that fancy computer of yours."

Actually there were dozens. Hundreds. What started out as a photo essay on the invasion of the water hyacinth had steered her to the overpopulation of the nutria, ravenous orange-toothed mammals who eat a quarter of their body weight in plants each day. Then she'd moved on to studying the people trapping and eating the big rodents. For three years now she'd been documenting the lives of the families of the deep swamp. She met children who'd seen no one but relatives until she showed up. Women who hadn't left their own dry square of ground in years. It had taken most of the first year just to find them and gain their trust. In the last eighteen months they'd been showing up at her place, a silent canoe with an equally silent man asking to see the photos, a teenager in a jon boat inviting her to a baptism.

Last year she'd sat in a deputy's skiff, while a team searched for a missing teenaged boy. Tina knew that the real terror of dragging for a body wasn't there in the water. It was at the water's edge, in the faces of the mothers who hardened their jaws and cussed the dang fool who hadn't come home, while their eyes reflected the waning hope that he'd come loping in the back way any minute, unharmed, so she could beat the tar out of him. Yes, Tina had photos.

"Point taken. No, I'm not planning to off myself," Tina said, though she could not at this moment promise.

Mary Jo sighed.

"I thought you were going to get out some more.

Looks like you slept in those clothes."

"I did. But before you go all sidekick on me, I went to town yesterday. Tried again. I had two bags of mail."

"So far so good," Mary Jo said.

"And outside the post office, some old woman snatched up her dog and spit at my feet."

"At them or on them?"

"It matters? At them. Three times!"

"Warding off evil. Did she say anything? Did you?"

"No and no. I came straight home to bed. Slept until six."

Mary Jo turned her chair toward Tina.

"You know this isn't your fault."

"The spitting?"

"No, the deaths. The universe isn't punishing you by killing people."

"And you know this how?"

"Trust me. It doesn't work that way."

"How does it work, then, Mary Jo? Some grand plan? A familial expiration date?"

"What have your spirit guides been telling you?"

"Quiet as Silent Bob."

"Give them a chance, Tina. In order to hear them, you have to listen."

It seemed like listening was all she'd been doing lately. The voices in her head told her to get out of Dodge. Abandon this freelance work. Get a job with a studio. A New York magazine. Shoot fashion models or charity events. But she never got further than an internet search before she'd find herself distracted by a gator's moan or the flash of a heron or her own numb wrist from cradling her chin on her work table. It wasn't just inertia. She was anchored here.

"Promise me," Mary Jo shut her truck door and

reached for Tina's hand through the open window. "Promise you'll do something today. It's time."

Mary Jo was right. It was time to get back to work. Tina poured another cup of coffee and dumped the first bag of mail onto her work table on the porch. The sorting was somehow comforting and easier than she thought. Most of the mail she shredded for compost. She scanned in a few checks with her phone to make a bank deposit and set up folders for two new assignments. The obvious cards of condolence she set aside in an empty flowerpot. She carried the bag of shredding out back to her composter. Jason had laughed at her the whole time she assembled the rotating barrel she bought to make her own dirt.

"A waste of your hard-earned cash," he said. "The bayou is one big composter. Look around."

"I have," she told him. "Your big composter is digesting whatever is dragged in here, but I don't want my tomato plants sucking up who knows what."

"Like the crayfish you eat don't do that."

She waggled a crescent wrench at him. "I don't eat the green poop part," she said. And despite his teasing she fed the composter, and filled bastion baskets with rich soil, and grew her vegetables above ground, away from the brackish water and its microbes. In time Jason took over most of the weeding and watering, and the bounty on their kitchen table made it into salads, and pastas, and skewers of grilled kabobs and stir fries. She hadn't been out here since Jason died, weeks ago now.

The green composter stood on sturdy legs in the sun. Tina gave the turning barrel's handle a good crank, then opened the metal sliding door. It was good and hot inside, just like it was supposed to be. She dumped in the shredded paper, then spun the handle a few more times to mix it in. In this heat it would take hardly any time to digest the paper.

While she was out here, she might as well survey the damage her neglect had done to the garden. Her sandals crunched oyster shells as she walked the path between the raised beds, but where she expected weeds and wilted plants she saw a perfectly-tended garden. Her tomatoes were staked, beefy red and green fruit hanging from supported vines as high as she was tall. Beans on the bush, plump okra, zucchini big as a man's arm, and not a weed in sight. No overripe or rotting vegetables, either. Perfect. She shivered as if a cloud had passed overhead, blocking out the sun. It looked as good as . . . as it ever had. As good as when Jason was here.

Tina looked around, looking for what, exactly, she didn't know. A sign? A glimpse of Jason? Some proof this was real, and all the rest a dream: the log truck, the sheriff at the screen door, the funeral, the copper urn. She broke off a sprig of rosemary and rubbed it between her fingers. This was real. And the tomato she picked was ripe, her thumb and forefinger making a perfect dent in the side as she bit into the smooth skin. She finished off the tomato in three bites. Its juice made yellow-red rivulets down the inside of her wrist. She turned her shirt into a basket, filling it with tomatoes and beans and peas. She stuck a zucchini under each arm and waddled into the house, laden like a Diego Rivera flower vendor. She dumped the lot on the kitchen table and rushed into the bedroom, hoping. But the urn with Jason's ashes was still there.

∞

Tina opened the ribbed aluminum case that held her favorite camera. She lifted the digital SLR to her face. It balanced her, the flat of the body in her palm, the weight of the lens against her fingertips. Her first camera, the one her dad sent her from Iraq, had felt just this way. Behind the lens she was safe. Not everyone understood that. Particularly her mother.

"How can you enjoy the scenery if that stupid camera is always in your face?" Her mother was stretched out on a blue canvas chair outside her condo in St. Martin, a book on her lap.

"I *am* enjoying it. These kids are such hams," Tina said, her camera trained on a pack of local boys playing king of the mountain on a swim platform in the bay. They were a tangle of limbs and glistening hair surrounded by an infinite turquoise blue.

Here in the bayou there was no blue water, but it was clear. Unless it was green. Or brown. It changed with the movement of the tide, the alligators that jostled the silt, the algae that bloomed or sank. Tina followed a ripple in the water with her viewfinder. She zoomed in on a nutria gliding toward her dock. It settled in on a nest of vines and yawned, flashing its orange front teeth.

"Don't go birthing your babies right there, momma," Tina whispered. "It's cursed ground." She snapped the shutter as the nutria yawned again. It lifted its head, but when an echoing thud sounded from behind the house, it slipped under the water, beneath a boat Tina didn't recognize.

From the corner of the house she heard the thumping again, and a boy no more than three feet tall stood with his legs apart lobbing dirt clods at the composter.

"Hey, cut it out!" Tina said.

He opened his left hand and let a handful of dirt fall to the ground. His head tilted down, but his eyes were wide, staring at her. She recognized him by his blue eyes. She'd only photographed one family with blue-eyed children—the

Brissettes. His first name escaped her.

"How'd you get here? Where's your momma?" Tina asked him.

He just toed the ground with a bare foot and hung his head.

"That your boat?"

He nodded.

"He's with me." A teenaged boy stepped from behind the tomato plants with a split-oak basket half-filled with vegetables. Her vegetables.

He followed her eyes to the basket, and he lifted his chin, his eyes proud beneath the brim of his baseball cap.

"We'll pay you . . ."

She shook her head. Robbie. That's the older boy. She had been there when their brother Paul had been pulled from the water.

"We ain't thieves."

"I know. Robbie, isn't it?" She remembered their mother standing at the water's edge, clutching her cotton blouse as if it was her only hold on reality. "How is your momma doing?"

"She done sent us here."

"You've been taking care of my garden." Tina felt her throat closing up, a precursor to tears.

"Yes'm, what with your loss and all. It don't pay to let food go to waste."

"Please. Take whatever. Anything you can use." Tina wiped her eyes with her forearm. "And thanks."

Robbie nodded, all business now. "Cole, get back to weeding them beans."

Tina wiped her eyes with a paper towel, then ran it over her neck. She was sweating and shaking and crying all at once. She leaned on the edge of the kitchen sink with her elbows and ran lukewarm water over the underside of her wrists. Eulalie, that was the boys' mother's name. Tina stood with her when the drag boat-turned-hearse idled away, out of sight, then finally out of sound. Eulalie insisted Tina and the deputy come inside for a glass of sweet tea, and they sat at the kitchen table, the oilcloth's pattern long faded from sun and scrubbing. Outside, Robbie, man of the house by default, knocked a log of firewood against a tree, again and again, the echo rushing over still water and back. Cole crouched on the porch, his T-shirt stretched over his knees like a tent and his hat pulled low. Inside the cabin was spare but immaculate, open shelves and walls covered with the trappings of men.

"They'll do an autopsy. See why he died," the deputy took a pull on his tea. "After, you want I should take him over with Pete?"

Eulalie nodded. A strand of hair loose from her ponytail bounced on her jaw. She swept it behind her ear and stood. At the door she looked down at Cole.

"Just the two left," she said. "There won't be more."

At the boat ramp, Tina asked about Pete.

"Her husband. Cancer got him a few months back. Not the first young'un she's lost either."

"How many?"

"You know, girl? I lost count."

∞

Tina thought the whole "capture your soul with a camera" thing was some third world myth, conjured up by westerners who tramped into jungles and deserts in search of knowledge or wealth. A hat trick, no different than her grandpa's lame slapstick game of "got your nose." The voodoo priestess she followed for a week for a photo essay checked her lipstick in the shine of a silver bracelet before allowing Tina a shot. Even she told Tina the bayou families would be afraid.

"The camera, it's bad magic," she said. Then she asked for prints for free.

The families were camera shy, Tina learned, but it wasn't the camera. It was the stranger behind the lens. The outsider. No different than the Kentucky farm families she shot in college or the Cheyenne she met one summer. Superstition was the real myth. They had no call to fear boogie men or voodoo chants; they saw for themselves what the bayou could dish up.

Tina pulled up a photo index on her computer. The Brissette file opened to the photos of the search for Paul, what she'd hoped were discreet shots of the family in crisis. She scrolled until she found what she was looking for—a family portrait shot the year before. Eulalie stood with Pete on the porch, his arm around her waist, the boys seated in front with scrubbed faces and slicked down hair. Their hands were still, "for a change," Eulalie had joked. Tina hit print.

Jason smiled at her from a silver frame. Their wedding. Too precious? Too soon? She picked up a rustic cypress frame with a photo from their housewarming. The two of them, a bottle of champagne at the doorway. She hugged it to her chest.

The boys walked by the porch, zucchini poking out of their basket like bread loaves.

"Wait!" She rapped on the porch door. "Don't go yet."

She swapped the portrait for the wedding photo in its frame and spit-polished it with the hem of her T-shirt, a mirror of silver, her own face repeated in a beveled edge.

Cole sat in the boat, his hand wrapped around the dock-cleated bow line.

"For your momma." Tina handed the framed photo

to Robbie.

Cole scrambled to look at it. "I want to see!" The boat rocked.

"Careful, Cole," Robbie said. He ran a finger over the glass and pulled off his hat, then his shirt, spreading it across the bench seat beside him. He wrapped the picture in his shirt and placed it under the middle seat. His eyes met Tina's. He nodded. Cole pulled in the bow line, and Robbie swung the boat toward home.

The reflection of the cypress wobbled in their wake. Tina dumped the water from the motor cover and set it in her truck bed. When Mary Jo came next she'd ask for help loading the motor in her truck. As the water stilled, the nutria paddled back and settled in under the dock.

NIBBLING AT THE BLOODSTAINS

This girl moves like she's underwater, practicing for the mermaid show at Weeki Wachee or something. What I really want to do is grab my sunflower seeds and water bottle off the counter and run out the door. Let mermaid girl keep my $18.21 in change, put the cash in the pocket of that massive company smock that hangs on her pointed shoulders like a poncho and later buy a six-pack or some milk for her kids and never make a peep if the cops come asking.

Here I stand, though, waiting, watching, because she reminds me of my daughter, Melissa, a rescuer, the weight of the world on a narrow frame. There's a cross dangling from the chain around her neck, and not a plain one either, but one of those Catholic ones with Jesus stuck on there like that's how he'd like to be remembered, all nailed up and nearly naked. No, this girl would run after me, leave a note with my complete description "in case the poor woman comes back for her change."

My silver-blue-haired grandma would have handed over exact change to begin with, paying for a dozen aspirin with a nickel and two pennies and slipping the brown and yellow tin into her pocketbook, giving me the empty one. I packed it with dimes. I was six. She was sixty. Now I'm that combined. Sixty-six going on nothing if I don't keep moving.

The girl waits for me to stick out my palm, and I raise my right arm but substitute my left, like a kid playing games. She starts with the penny, layers on the dimes, the bills. She counts with her mouth, just like Melissa's husband Brandon does. Did.

"And twenty," she says. She smiles and bumps the register closed with the heel of her hand.

Bottle sweat stings the rope burn on my right palm.

"Have a good day, and God bless," she says. I open the door with my hip and set off down the road to where my skiff is tied to a stake on the bank of the Okeechobee Waterway.

The air tastes like asphalt, as if the squiggly heat waves from the pavement coat my tongue when I inhale. I find a patch of shade under a trio of Christmas palms. Even in the shade the humidity holds me close, comforts me. The palms rustle from a breeze far over my head. At my nursery, only a few miles away by water, the rows of palms planted a year apart alternately catch the wind like this when it rises off the big lake. Will Melissa stand there today, listening to the wind play their fronds like harp strings?

I dump seeds in my mouth directly from the tube. I haven't eaten since lunch yesterday. I need salt, water. I chew the seeds to pulp. A pickup shows up on the horizon, fuzzy and shimmering. I step behind a tree trunk, even though its diameter is half mine. Age has spread my hips, and my shoulders are broad beneath my work shirt. My sun hat, rolled no bigger than a bratwurst, is snug in a pants pocket. I pat my waistband out of habit, but my gloves aren't there. They are on the bottom of the canal, somewhere west of Lake Hopcochee where I dropped them overboard last night. I figure catfish are picking at the frayed canvas. Nibbling at the bloodstains: mine, his. The story problem is this: if 200 pounds of flesh falls fifteen feet at the end of 115 feet of rope on a four-inch pulley, how much friction will it generate? Enough to burn through a pair of heavy duty work gloves and rip a bloody trench into an old woman's hands.

My boat is where I left it. I yank the metal stake from the scrub and carry the line down the bank into the skiff. It's the same rope, practically, as I use in the shop: twelve strands woven together, not too much stretch, abrasion resistant. To the arborist it's a rope; to the mariner it's a line, but they serve the same purpose. They tie up things you want to stay put, and they keep your loved ones safe. That was the plan, anyway.

Just after two o'clock I reach the Caloosahatchee River that connects the waterway to the Sound, and I motor past the Ft. Myers bridges and into a nearly full marina, a world away from the lake that was my home. Here fancy trawlers with perfect canvas sport flat screen TVs. The sailboats are at least 32-footers. Behind me are million-dollar condos no one is buying, even though a flapping banner says they're now only $359,000. Ten out of 200 are sold I read somewhere. It's the market, supposedly. That's what Brandon blamed for his failure in real estate, not his drinking, certainly, or that look in his eye that contradicted that capped-tooth smile he whitened with overnight trays from the drugstore. Couldn't tell by my business. People never stopped wanting more shade, or more oranges, or more bougainvillea. Brandon had no eye for landscaping. No, his eye was on the brass ring, or more likely the belly ring barely visible under the silk blouse of our biggest corporate buyer. Meeting clients and marketing was what I hired him to do. But as much as Melissa prayed otherwise, he was really a meat market kind of guy.

"If he could just make a go of it," she told me. "Get his confidence back. He might not need . . ." She twisted a curly strand of hair into a corkscrew.

"You know," she said. "Those others."

There was a parade of them, and as each one was discovered, or blurted out in a drunken rage, I saw Melissa square her shoulders, set her jaw, and narrow her eyes in determination.

Melissa could coax a neglected seedling to sprout leaves or an abused and abandoned kitten to eat from her hand. She tried her magic on Brandon, but unlike the seedling that grew to shower her with peaches or the cat who dropped furry field mouse heads at her feet, Brandon kept up his nefarious ways. No, he flat out defied her, and it was me who tired of waiting for him to change. I watched her shoulders grow thin, her eyes draw back in their sockets, and that determined jaw tremble more often than not. Melissa saw it as her personal failure and tried harder. Not me.

Two men work the condo grounds. One, on a stand-up mower, spins circles around a young azalea. Another sprays impatiens with a hose in full sun. I step off the brick walkway into the grass, then stop myself. Not my crew. Not by a long shot.

The harbormaster's nose is in a book when I enter the office. The cold air catches my tonsils unaware. I cough.

He looks up.

"What can I do you for?" He puts his book down

open, spine up.

"That fresh coffee?" I point to a pot on top of the file cabinet.

"Help yourself." He stretches in his chair, a man in no hurry. A fisherman, no doubt.

I sip coffee. The bulletin board has snapshots of men holding big fish, some business cards, boats for sale, and one for rent. I watch minnows in the bait tank and survey a wall of lures. Five reels of line are mounted underneath. A red reel just like mine.

A young girl in a bikini walks by as I carry my coffee outside. Her sarong is tied low on her hips, and a belly ring sparkles against her tan abdomen.

The buyer had a belly ring just like that, but a pale and puffy stomach. Did she sneak back in last night to get the rest of her clothes or did she pretend nothing happened? Make believe her lover's mother-in-law hadn't found them pressed together on a bale of burlap in the barn, Brandon's white butt lit purple in the bug zapper's light? I had tossed her abandoned shoe, a black Jimmy Choo with silver stars, into the baler with Brandon before I encased him in the net like a Christmas tree headed for the top of an Escalade. Let him sober up hanging from the boom of my truck, an evil-doer captured by Spider Man. When he saw his philandering, naked self hanging fifteen feet above the ground in a tree net, maybe he'd morph into a new man.

I squint in the sun. A man in a green shirt waves a clipboard and points a pencil stub at an ailing palm tree harbor side of the closest condo tower. I see the problem: a load of mulch piled around the trunk. Between the heat and trapped moisture, the tree will die from the ground up. The workers take a shovel and tamp down the mulch, compacting it.

"No, no, no!" Clipboard man gets on his knees and pulls mulch away from the trunk.

"I wonder who made the first mulch volcano?" I say. He looks up at me and shakes his head. The base of the tree is exposed. It's wet and soft. I kneel down and prod the bark with my fingers, looking for any hint of the telltale white wafer from gandoderma butt rot. It's felling palms all over Florida, and there's no cure.

"Looks like it's just heat and moisture," I say. "No gandoderma."

I sit back on my heels and look him in the eye.

"She'll need some looking after," I say. "Not to mention the others. And the crepe myrtles? Could use an artist."

"Done this before?" he asks.

I nod, but it doesn't come close to how I feel. It's all I know. It's what I love. It's all I have left.

"Ten an hour to start. No benefits, but it's steady. Forty hours a week or more, if you've got the time."

I nod again.

"I've got some paperwork in the truck," he says, then stops when I shake my head.

"I'd rather not," I say. "An old grandmother like me prefers cash."

He looks past me to his workers digging at another palm, then back to me. I see him take in my chopped off hair, the lines the sun has sketched into my face and neck, and the slick red line of skin across my palm.

"Okay, *Abuelita*, long as you didn't kill someone," he smiles.

I plant my sun hat on my head, pulling it tight so the brim will shade the tip of my nose. I smile from my personal shade.

"At least not on purpose," I say.

He laughs a big belly laugh, then fans himself with his clipboard.

"Tomorrow, seven sharp. I'll get you the drawings. You set the priorities."

We shake hands. I wince, and he tosses me a pair of gloves.

I grab a fistful of soil and test it for moisture. It smells of the ocean, and sunlight, and fish.

I tuck the new gloves in my waistband and visit the harbormaster. By morning my skiff will be transformed into a dinghy, a fresh stripe of paint just below her gunwale and a paint-stenciled name that matches my rented sailboat will disguise it for now.

At dusk, a bartender squirts two shots of Cuervo Gold into a blender at a bar on the boardwalk. I hadn't counted on Brandon getting sick and choking on the tequila and whatever else his stomach heaved up. I let out the rope to bring him down fast and steady, but he thrashed around, and I lost control. He gained momentum, and the rope ran through the pulley and across my palms. It didn't stop until he hit the concrete floor, the net stretched tight against his skin and a four-and-a-half inch Jimmy Choo spike heel sunk deep in the middle of his chest.

The sky is red before night. From the cockpit I see whirlpools of surface-feeding fish. I let an ice cube melt in my palm, coating the burn. Yesterday I was the boss. Today I'm the little grandmother. Tomorrow, maybe I'm the mother Melissa forgives, the one who forced her to turn a nurturing eye on herself for once.

The tide tugs at my moorings, but I won't escape to the sea. I'm anchored to the land as securely as these lines wrap the dock cleats. My roots run deep. My rhizomes, underground runners themselves, will take nourishment from the soil until they're strong enough to surface once more.

BORDERING ON SAINTHOOD

Derwin Hooper stomped on what he thought would be the last cockroach to dance around his kitchen, but as it turned out, the last waltz was for Derwin.

"Die, you mother!" Derwin yelled. He mashed the crusty invader against the linoleum floor with a size 13 Wolverine and ripped the tape off the top of the last of a six-pack of aerosol bug foggers. The other five were already spewing their grey smoke into the air in the eight-by-twelve foot kitchen. Derwin rubbed his burning eyes with the sleeve of his "Kiss Me I'm Drunk" T-shirt and accidentally poked fogger number four with a steel toe. The canister skittered through the swirling cloud on the floor to the base of the hot water heater like a hockey puck over fresh ice into an unguarded net. Derwin coughed. It was the last thing he would do.

Carol Ann became a widow while sitting in the drive-thru at Fat Boy's Burgers and Bikes. She'd ordered the beefy V-twin burger for Derwin and the grilled Biker Chick fillet for herself, with extra fries. Her stomach was churning away at the Mountain Dew she'd downed for breakfast. She'd refused to cook a thing as long as the kitchen was full of roaches. Derwin was full of promises, but his empty stomach finally won him over. Since he was taking steps to fix the problem, Carol Ann was springing for carry-out.

The town fire siren wound up to a scream, and Carol Ann checked her watch. It was only 11:30. Too early for the noon signal. The sliding window on the side of the restaurant opened, and Darlene Applegate hunkered her shoulders diagonally in the square opening so she could get closer to Carol Ann's Camaro. Carol Ann started to reach for her food, but Darlene was empty-handed.

"You might want to get on home, Carol Ann. Bobby tells me that firetruck's headed your way." Darlene's husband, Bobby, was a dispatcher for the county. As tuned in as she was, Darlene might as well have been carrying a radio herself.

"Not without my food, Darlene. I already paid," Carol Ann said.

Darlene clucked her tongue and disappeared inside. Carol Ann ran through the gears with the clutch in while she waited. If this was fast food, Carol Ann would hate to see how long it took Darlene to serve up a sit-down dinner. Darlene came back and handed over a brown paper bag with the burgers and drinks.

Carol Ann rummaged through the bag, looking for condiments.

"Got any extra ketchup in there? Derwin freaks out if there's not enough ketchup."

Carol Ann had finished half her fries by the time she turned onto her street. She couldn't get near her own house for all the cars. They hadn't had this much company since their wedding. It looked like every volunteer firefighter came on his own instead of riding on the truck. There were five pickup trucks with blue lights still flashing, and there was an ambulance. Sitting on her lawn was the big firetruck, along with the Chief's Hummer the town had gotten with its homeland security money. Fire chief Don Spradley stood with one foot on the passenger side runningboard, smoking cigarettes with two other firemen in T-shirts and yellow-suspendered pants. Two more, wearing their buttoned-up canvas coats, double-teamed a hose spraying water at what once was her kitchen. Actually, from where she stood in the front yard with her now-greasy burger bag in her hand, there wasn't much left of the whole north side of her place. It didn't seem like much of a fire, but something had torched Derwin's F-150, at least the side she could see. He always parked it in the drive close to the kitchen door. He was going to be pissed. She was surprised she didn't hear him ranting and raving.

She finished her fries before the Chief noticed she was there. He was taller than her daddy, which was saying something, and he was nearly as wide as Carol Ann was tall. He walked all stiff-legged, and he wheezed when he breathed. Falling off a ladder and fighting rural fires for thirty years will do that to you. He wiped his face on his bare arm. There was a white ring from his eyebrows up where his hat had been. Below that his face was gray as ashes with black charcoal smudges.

"Carol Ann," he began, then wheezed into a cough. He had one of those long-time smoker's coughs that started way down somewhere and worked its way up. She handed him a napkin from the burger bag.

"Lordy, Carol Ann. I'm trying to give you the bad news, and here you're helping me," he said. He stuffed the napkin in his pocket and wiped his forehead again.

33

"If you're fixin' to tell me my house is half gone, I can see that for myself, Don."

"It's not that, Carol Ann. It's Derwin." He put a hand on Carol Ann's shoulder. She wondered if whatever he had in his lungs was catching. "I'm afraid Derwin didn't make it out. Well, he made it out, but not really. I mean . . . well, for god's sakes, Carol Ann, he blew himself up. Things are just laying all over the place back there."

Carol Ann was just going to let that little bit of information slide right on by for now. She wasn't going to let it into her brain to start bouncing around like a ping pong ball. No, she was going to just let it sit there, like a name tag on her chest or a sticky note on the calendar until she was ready to deal with it. It might be there for a while.

"There wasn't much of a fire. I got them spraying things down good just in case," he said.

She stared at Derwin's truck. Just underneath the passenger door were twisted pots and pans. A kitchen chair was shoved between the front tire and the wheel well.

"Carol Ann," the Chief said. "You hear me? You okay?"

"I was just getting us some food," she said. "Couldn't leave him alone for a second. Couldn't even kill a roach without supervision."

"How, Carol Ann? With those fogger cans?"

"Bombs," she said. "They call them bombs."

"Who'd a thought that could really happen?" the Chief said. He scratched his head and hollered over to the two guys over by what was left of the house. He was using his official words that Carol Ann always wondered if he learned in fireman school or from watching cop shows on the TV.

"Hey, canvas the scene for any of those fogger cans for bugs. Looks like he was setting them off," the Chief said.

"Them foggers did this?" Danny Virgin said. He was sifting through the rubble with a rake. He had a cigarette hanging out of his mouth. "Who'd a thought that could really happen?"

Carol Ann looked at Danny then back to the Chief. She just shook her head.

The EMTs gathered up what they could of Derwin and put his various parts in a black plastic bag with a zipper. It wasn't like on TV where a whole team of people with expensive cameras and tight shirts picked up little pieces of glass and fingernails with tweezers. One of two town cops walked around the place for a few minutes and told Carol Ann he was sorry about her loss. Carol Ann sat on the shiny silver floor at the back of the ambulance, dangling her feet. The Chief put a blanket around her shoulders, but it was hot. She draped it over her lap and tried to work a loose thread back into the weave with her fingers. It kept popping back out, no matter how many times she tried. If it was her own blanket, she'd just bite the string off with her teeth. But it wasn't. No telling what that blanket had been on.

"Carol Ann," one of the EMTs said real quiet but quite close to her ear. She jumped up and dropped the blanket. Her rear end and both her feet were numb.

"We need to get in there now," he said. They had arranged the body bag on a folding stretcher. She ran her palm over the top of the bag. It was warm.

"So that's it? That's him?" she said.

"Best we can tell, Carol Ann," he said. She knew where he had sat in study hall, but she didn't know his name. "I'm real sorry, you know." He closed the double back doors of the ambulance one at a time and walked around to the front. Derwin didn't really need any company in the back at this point. The EMTs drove off slow with their siren making little yipping sounds instead of the long wails it does when there's the remote possibility of saving the passenger. Carol Ann watched them until they turned the corner.

The last of the firefighters rolled up their hoses and lugged them back to the truck. The Chief stretched yellow plastic tape around the yard, hooking it to the side of the house with a staple gun.

"That's not for me, is it?" Carol Ann asked. "I got stuff to do in there."

"Not right now, Carol Ann. Not until I get a fire inspector out here. It's not safe anyway. Least not yet. We turned off the gas and the 'lectric. You got someplace to go?"

Carol Ann ticked off the possibilities in her head, but not one of them made any sense to her. No, she was going to sit right here for now. She nodded at Don. It wasn't really a lie. She did have someplace to go. She just wasn't going.

A Honda Accord skidded into the front yard, tearing patches of grass out by the roots and coming to a stop just street-side of Carol Ann's favorite peony bush. Her mother-in-law Peggy jumped out, leaving the door open and the key alarm dinging.

"Where is he? Where's my baby?" Peggy shouted. She had one hand hooked in her hair and the other back across her forehead like she was going to faint.

"Now, Peggy," the Chief said, moving slowly toward her with his arms out front, "just calm down, now, honey. It's going to be all right."

"Donnie, where's my baby?" she said, staring hard at Carol Ann, who just stood there.

"He's gone, Peggy," he said. "Your Derwin's gone."

Peggy staggered. The Chief caught her underneath her arms and held her upright. She slumped against him and started to wail, like one of those women on the news from some other country with chanting in the background. Peggy's background noise was the dinging key alarm from the Accord. While the Chief patted Peggy on the back and filled her in as to the circumstances of her son's death, Carol Ann walked over to Peggy's car and shut the door with her hip. She punched her toe at a patch of grass to see if she could smooth it back over. No luck.

Peggy continued to cry but slid one eye over to Carol Ann. It wasn't that Carol Ann thought Peggy shouldn't or wouldn't be upset about Derwin. Heck, she had a right to be as upset as anyone, next to Carol Ann herself, of course. It was just how she went about things. Derwin called her "the drama queen." He used to say that's what he liked about Carol Ann, her being so different from his momma. Carol Ann thought Peggy just put on that excited act for attention, but she never told that to Derwin. It didn't matter to her one way or another what Peggy's intentions were.

Carol Ann, she just took things in stride. As far as Carol Ann was concerned it was the only way to be in this town where there were always boys jumping off cliffs into the river, shooting each other with BB guns for the fun of it, or playing chicken with their cars on the old highway at night out by the drag strip where the real drivers counted down the pole for the green. The drag strip radio ads had an echo, "Be-be-be there-there-there. Sun-sun day-day. Raceway Park. Be-be there-there." If you half-listened it almost sounded like "be-be ware-ware," but that would never occur to the boys hopped up on testosterone and the fumes of burning rubber who floored their Mustangs and Nissans on a count of three, flying with no chute. Derwin was more likely to be found under a hood than looking over one. His best buddy, Trevor, was always blowing up his engine or something equally tragic, and Derwin was the one up to his elbows in grease with a trouble light swinging above his head and a socket wrench stuck through a belt loop. Carol Ann's big sister Annie was in love with Trevor, and Carol Ann just came along for the ride. After a while, people just considered Derwin and Carol Ann a couple, and in a town that small, that was good enough.

"I drove like a bat out of hell to get here," Peggy said, "soon as I heard."

"We noticed," Carol Ann said. "Me and my grass. A few more feet and they'd a had to get the Jaws of Life to get you out of my bedroom."

The Chief unwrapped Peggy from his torso. "I got to get back and call the fire inspector."

He put his hand on Carol Ann's shoulder for the second time that day. "You need anything, you call me," he said.

"Peggy," he nodded to Derwin's mom and limped to his Hummer and hauled himself up the running board into the seat.

Peggy eyed the bags from Fat Boy's Carol Ann had put on the porch.

"I rushed all the way over from Princeton. Didn't even stop for lunch," Peggy said. Carol Ann sat on the porch and opened a bag. She pulled out her chicken sandwich and munched a few of Derwin's fries.

"You going to eat all that?" Peggy asked.

Carol Ann pushed the open bag over toward Peggy. The porch boards squeaked when she sat down.

"Got any extra ketchup?" Peggy rummaged around in the bag, and then stuck her finger inside the bun on Derwin's sandwich. "Pretty cold."

"Well, my microwave may be out back somewhere," Carol Ann said.

Peggy started crying again. Carol Ann re-wrapped

her own sandwich and put it in the bag. She couldn't swallow right, and she wasn't even crying. Peggy seemed to manage somehow, maybe by washing it down with a drink.

"Kind of watery," Peggy said.

"Ice melted," Carol Ann said. "I made tea . . . "

They both looked toward the back of the house. Peggy cried some more.

"Who'd a thought that would happen?" Peggy said when her shoulders stopped shaking. She blew her nose on a napkin from the bag.

Maybe the people who wrote the directions, Carol Ann said to herself. To Peggy she said, "It says on the box to turn off any appliances with a pilot light."

"So?" Peggy said.

"So, there's a pilot light on the kitchen stove and on the water heater, and that's in the kitchen."

"Are you saying my boy couldn't read? He was good at readin'."

"He can read, Peggy. He don't bother to read anything like directions, but he can read just fine."

"Don't be bad mouthing him. He could read," Peggy said.

Carol Ann took in a deep breath and let it out real slow. She dumped her watered-down drink in a pot of geraniums at the corner of the porch. It wasn't Carol Ann who was the critical one, and it never had been. Carol Ann dealt in facts. If the roaches were in the kitchen, it wasn't sanitary to cook. It didn't matter to her if Derwin or one of his buddies dragged them in the house inside a cardboard case of fresh long necks or if she herself carried the eggs home in a paper grocery sack. What mattered is they were there, and they were multiplying. Derwin's mom, though, she would have cared plenty who brought the nasty creatures into the house. And once she knew? Pick, pick, pick. Derwin didn't say a thing that day Peggy told him he wasn't welcome at her dinner table unless he scrubbed the grease out from under his nails. Carol Ann could see with her own eyes that the stains were pretty much permanent. He used that liquidy paste cleaner and soap with real volcano lava, but his hands never came clean. Peggy's car ran just fine, though, thanks to those hands. At home that night Carol Ann kissed each finger, even though Derwin tried to pull them away. "They're all stained and rough, Carol Ann," he protested. She kissed them anyway, and rubbed them against her cheeks.

Peggy dug a pack of cigarettes out of her pocket and offered one to Carol Ann. Carol Ann shook her head.

"You know I quit," she said.

"I thought maybe you'd need one about now," Peggy said, inhaling deep inside somewhere.

Carol Ann felt like she had been smoking something awful. The air was not real smoky, but it had that fire smell even though it was mostly an explosion. It smelled like burnt food and insecticide. Her tongue tasted like bug spray. She dug another napkin out of the bag and wiped her tongue.

"Gross," Peggy said. She tapped her ashes onto the porch.

Carol Ann closed her eyes and leaned her head back against the side of the house. "Say it ain't so, Joe," she heard Derwin say somewhere inside her head. She and Derwin had watched *Eight Men Out* on DVD just last night. They usually picked up a pizza and rented a movie on Friday nights, but last night they watched one they owned. Derwin had almost every word memorized. She'd gotten him the DVD for Christmas because the VHS he had was taped off the TV and had commercials. This summer they wanted to go to Chicago and see a White Sox game. They weren't playing at Comiskey Park anymore, Derwin explained. That stadium was torn down in 1991. He had begged his parents to take him there before it was gone, but no dice. He was just six, so they didn't take him serious. Even then his baseball card collection meant as much to him as his Hot Wheels. They built New Comiskey, but then some phone company handed over $68 million to get it named after them. "That makes the hundred grand the Black Sox were to get seem like chump change," Derwin told her. She'd left those Chicago pamphlets she sent off for on the kitchen table when she went to pick up some lunch. She imagined them fluttering to the ground in the backyard or maybe into the bed of Derwin's truck. Say it ain't so.

"You call the insurance?" Peggy said.

Carol Ann shook her head. "I haven't left the place."

"Where's your cell phone, then?"

Carol Ann pointed at her car.

"You just going to leave it there?"

Carol Ann nodded. Peggy lit another cigarette.

For the most part the gawkers driving by slow didn't interrupt them. Carol Ann knew it was just people paying their respects. Darlene Applegate drove by after a while and hung half out the window of her Toyota. Carol Ann thought she must have a thing about hanging out windows. Darlene didn't say anything, just hung there for a while and then moved on. One car broke from the informal procession, though, and parked right in the drive behind the truck. The guy who got out had a badge hanging around his neck and a camera.

"You that fire inspector?" Peggy called from the porch.

"You expecting an inspector?" the man asked. He walked closer, right along the line of the police tape and put one foot up on the porch step. Carol Ann looked at his badge. It was just a business card hanging in a plastic case. The print was too little to read his name, but the *Herald-Dispatch* was on there in big print. Not so official after all.

"Ben Darnell, *Herald-Dispatch*."

"Peggy Hooper, mother of the deceased," Peggy said. She wiped crumbs from her lap with the back of her hand, then wiped her eyes. "This here's the widow, Carol Ann."

Carol Ann looked at Peggy. What, now she was in some episode of *Law and Order*? She'd seen the reporter before. He sometimes came in the hospital late at night, trying to talk to families. Sometimes he'd walk right over the floor Carol Ann had just washed, as if the "Wet Floor—Caution" signs were invisible. Maybe he was the one who couldn't read. He pulled a notepad out of his hip pocket and held it close to his eyes. He wrote right next to his face with his left hand. Then he looked at Carol Ann.

"With an 'e'?"

"No, 'y'. Like Peggy Lee," Peggy said.

"Who?"

Peggy looked crushed. Carol Ann shifted her weight. She felt like the whole house was pushing on her where she sat.

"Where have I seen you before?" he asked Carol Ann.

"Small town," she said. He continued to stare at her.

"You wouldn't happen to have a recent picture of your husband, would you, uh . . ." he looked at his notes, "Carol Ann?"

Carol Ann started to open the front door but stopped when she remembered what the Chief had said. What the heck, she thought. She put her shoulder to the door and went on in.

"You all stay there," she said from inside.

Her living room was usually dark and cool in the summer, but today it was anything but. The whole left wall, the one that connected to the kitchen, was gone. Carol Ann could see the F-150 and part of the backyard, too. Books and CDs and DVDs were thrown everywhere. Some looked good as new. Others were ripped or burned around the edges, and there was melted plastic stuck to the couch that looked like part of the TV. On the other side of the room, where Derwin had made her special shelf to hold her three Precious Moments statues and a glass frame with his best baseball card, things weren't so bad. The baseball card frame had some water on the front. She wiped it on her jeans. Looked like it was okay inside. Her statues were wet, too, and one was knocked over. The one from the wedding cake was cracked. The other two, one for each anniversary, would dry off just fine. She needed a bag to carry stuff in. She turned toward the kitchen but saw it wasn't there. She put the statues back on the shelf, shoved the baseball card and frame into the back waistband of her jeans and walked outside to the porch.

The reporter was sitting next to Peggy on the steps, writing fast, the notepad nearly resting on his nose.

Peggy was finishing a family story about Derwin rescuing the evil and overweight cat of an elderly neighbor. Somehow the psychotic cat became a frightened and helpless kitten. *How'd you think that cat got up in that tree in the first place?* Carol Ann wanted to ask Peggy. *Derwin flung him up there, that's how.*

"He was always rescuing animals and bringing them home," Peggy said. "He was good with little children, too. And an excellent reader." She dropped an eyebrow toward Carol Ann with that one.

The reporter turned to Carol Ann.

"No pictures," she said. She leaned against the side

of the house. The deep frame cut into her back a bit. It was the first thing she'd felt besides numbness and heat in a few hours.

"He was a real animal person. He used to fix the van for the animal shelter for free," Peggy added.

This morning Derwin was just Carol Ann's hungry husband who was finally going to do something about those roaches. Now to hear Peggy tell it, he was practically bordering on sainthood.

"Chief Spradley tells me those bug bombs caused this," he said. "Who'd have thought that could happen?"

Carol Ann shrugged.

"What would you want to say to the people who make those things if you could talk to them right now?"

"I think they should be outlawed," Peggy said. "I think they should pay for killing my baby." She started crying again.

"So, you'd start a crusade to get them banned?"

"That's it," Peggy said. "A crusade."

Carol Ann crossed the porch and opened her car door. She set the baseball card in its frame on the floorboard in the back. Derwin had given her this car for a wedding present. It took him almost a year to fix it up. They drove to Louisville and Cincinnati to get parts without even taking time to see the ballparks. Everything was original. Like the two of them. She slipped into the driver's seat that Derwin had mounted at just the right height for her and pushed in the clutch. One late night she sat on a little rolling stool in the garage, smoking and sipping a beer, watching Derwin work on her car. He dropped a bolt that rolled underneath the car, and when she went to retrieve it she cut her arm on something sharp by the new bumper. She stopped the blood with a shop rag, but Derwin took her over to the sink and washed the cut and put on a Band-Aid.

"Cover it up, and it won't hurt any more. Don't even look at it until it gets its scab," he said, kissing the bandage.

The Camaro's engine hummed in front of her, muted, but powerful. "She's just like you," Derwin used to tell her, grinning.

"Carol Ann," Peggy hollered. "What do you think you're doing?"

In the rearview mirror, Carol Ann saw the reporter walking toward her. She rotated the mirror up to face the roof and put her in gear. The car ran like she always did, the gasoline pouring into the carburetor fueling the pistons in their cylinders that moved with precision to carry Carol Ann wherever she wanted to go.

About a mile from town she saw the Chief's Hummer coming toward her. He stopped in the middle of the road and backed up. She did the same.

"Need anything, Carol Ann?"

She shook her head and adjusted the rearview mirror.

"When you coming back?"

Carol Ann started to shrug, then changed her mind.

"When the scab forms," she said.

Don looked toward Carol Ann, but she knew he was looking past her, to thirty years of flames and soot and falling rafters and bodies beyond recognition.

"Till then," he said, and he pulled away. She did the same.

SIDE OF BACON

Marva knew that the holidays were not a good time to ask her husband for a favor. That's why she was wedged here at the bottom of the basement stairs, imprisoned between a wall of concrete blocks and the sturdy legs of a solid oak pie safe. Who'd have thought the banister would give way like that?

It's not that she was blaming Dale for her predicament. After all, she was the one who wanted the pie safe moved. It was fine with Dale to leave it in the corner of the kitchen where it had stood for the seven years since her grandmother gave up housekeeping and Marva had "just the place" for the family heirloom. Until after New Year's, Dale wasn't going to want to deal with one more thing, especially anything that involved heavy lifting. He moved things around all day: ornate wrought iron bird cages, aquariums the size of couches, and truckloads of premium dog food.

"All I want is to take off these shoes," Dale said last night when Marva offered to fry some eggs.

"How about a sandwich? Or a piece of pie?"

"No," he said, with a little force. Marva backed off. He slumped on the couch, his stocking feet on a throw pillow on the coffee table. In a few minutes he would climb the stairs and crawl into bed. He had been like this since Thanksgiving when the mall extended its hours. "Twelve Days of Christmas—Bah Humbug" screamed the ads in the fancy curlz MT typeface Marva recognized from her own computer-generated Christmas cards. The mall promised shoppers not twelve but thirty days of Christmas with all stores open fifteen hours a day, twelve on Sunday. That was no big deal for the card shop next to Dale's store. A couple of passes with the feather duster and the store manager could turn the key that rolled up the grille door and greet the first customer of the day. Dale needed two hours to feed everyone, clean cages, straighten merchandise and mop the floors. And that was if all his staff showed up. At closing there was feeding, more cleaning, and paperwork. How could she ask him to do extra chores at home?

Marva took inventory. The cabinet wasn't going anywhere. It was lodged between the fourth step from the bottom and the wall, the hand-chiseled oak leaves and acorns on the space between the legs making a perfect arc around her lower ribs like a child's high chair tray. She wiggled her toes. She imagined her bare feet as blue as Smurf skin, brushing up against the back of the 100-year-old oak. She hated wearing shoes in the house, even in December. She'd spent the afternoon in the kitchen where the oven kept her toasty. The cold was seeping though the concrete floor, past the fleecy lining of her sweatpants into her rear end. She swore her bones were cold, but at least they weren't broken. Her head hurt where it slammed against the wall when she dodged the falling pie safe. She didn't get impaled on the legs, but she didn't escape either. She ran her palm across the back of her head. The hairs tingled, like she'd slept crooked on big hair rollers. No blood, though. That was a good sign.

She pushed against the pie safe, but even with the wall at her back, it wouldn't budge. She wiggled her legs underneath the wood to no avail. She was stuck like an accused witch in stocks.

Upstairs in the kitchen the oven timer beeped. Three beeps, a pause, then three more. The cookies were done. She'd baked Dale's favorite molasses cookies. The last tray was in the oven when she decided to slip a rope around the banister to guide the safe down the steps into the basement. Multi-tasking was her specialty. Now one of her tasks was progressing without her. The series of beeps repeated.

The cozy smell of baking cookies turned into the acrid smell of burning molasses. Marva struggled against the furniture, throwing her body at the legs.

"Solid oak," her grandmother had told her. "Your great grandpa Jefferson built this." He made as few cuts as possible with his sharpest hand saw. They didn't call oak "hardwood" for nothing. He chiseled in the pattern. The front was all one piece, except for the doors. Those legs went all the way up.

The beeping was drowned out now by the smoke alarm. Marva tried pushing with her knees. Where's that adrenalin rush I'm supposed to get? she said to herself. If people could overturn cars to rescue people, why couldn't she toss this furniture to rescue her own self? She pushed until the muscles in her arms rebelled, and then she beat on the wood with her fists, the soft flesh reddening with every punch, the wood unyielding, until her bones felt bruised and her shirt was damp with tears. She took in the short shallow breaths of a whimpering child, then dried her face on her sleeves. *Get a grip*, she told herself. *There's got to be a way out of this.*

She imagined the cookies blackening in the oven, their bottoms scorching like burning cowpies from grass-fed bovines. Grass-fed cow poop was smokier than poop from desert-fed cows, according to Dale. She calculated it was only a matter of minutes until the cookies burst into flame, spreading from the oven to the wallpaper to the curtains. How long would it be before the deadly smoke slid down the now-disconnected banister to the basement? The smoke alarm's scream reverberated in her head. Just underneath she could hear the beep of the timer. Three, pause, three.

Marva knew that animals caught in traps would gnaw off their own legs to escape. One limb wouldn't do it in her case; she'd have to gnaw herself in half. What would a smart dog do in her place? Dale was always telling her stories about how animals knew more about survival and healing than most humans do. He said some dogs can smell cancer on humans. He called it "detecting chemical markers." He said they could smell breast cancer and lung cancer. Dale was going to be a vet, back when. The pet store, it was one of those unplanned things. A part-time job during college turned into a full-time one, and when old man McCracken decided to get out of the business, he made Dale an offer he would have been a fool to refuse. Marva coughed and covered her mouth. Her fingernails were blue. She spread her fingers and her hands shook. What was it in the smoke that killed you? Carbon monoxide?

She'd scream if there was anyone to answer. She was the one the other neighbors asked to sign for their packages or let in the furnace guy. What part of home-based business didn't they understand? But she did it anyway, making herself too busy to do anything but the pressing design work and her own household chores. She'd hoped to get back to her own work, her real work, not this commercial stuff. It was a little late now.

Not for Dale, though. Maybe he could take her life insurance payout and go to vet school. Get out of that mall. Unless the whole house burned down. Her life insurance policy was in her bottom left hand desk drawer, but she was pretty sure Dale didn't know that. She really should have gotten a safe deposit box. No telling what else they would lose in the fire. Besides her, of course. She should have taken training as a hospice volunteer. Then maybe she'd know how to prepare for whatever came next. It seemed a little late to start praying. Wasn't her life supposed to pass before her eyes? Her luck it wasn't her life that she was reviewing, but a list of undone tasks. Why should her brain work any differently facing death than it did every night facing sleep?

Her hips ached. From the cold? From sitting so still? Her hips used to ache from painting, on her feet for hours in a rented studio near campus. It was one large room, more like a glassed-in porch built to make the most of the available light, but she almost always worked at night, after class, after her job stocking shelves at the Piggly Wiggly, her feet as cold as they were now. She liked oversized canvas for the big sky of home. Bluer than glass cleaner or topaz or even her own eyes. Blue first, then the rusty brown rocky dirt as background for the tiniest flower or cactus needle or unturned stone. She painted sometimes on her tiptoes, sometimes in a squat. While the Midwestern sleet tapped at the windows like an unkindness of ravens, she warmed herself in the light of her paintings, drawing strength from the desert as it took shape under her brushes.

Leaving the studio at 2:00 one Sunday morning, her jeans a paint-spattered collage of blues and browns, she stopped at a campus waffle place for breakfast. She sat in a corner booth, warming her hands on a cup of coffee, watching the short order cook toss eggs and spin his spatula when the waitress brought her a plate of bacon.

"I didn't order any bacon," Marva said. The waitress pointed to three boys in a booth across the room. They looked her way and held their coffee cups in the air, like a toast.

"It's from them," the waitress said. She shrugged and stepped back to the end of the counter.

Marva picked up a piece of bacon. It was crisp and lean, just the way she liked it. She waved the piece at the boys, as if doffing a hat. They punched each other on the arms, the way boys do.

On the way out, she stopped at their table.

"So, what's the deal with the bacon?" she asked.

The one with the brown hair, who turned out to be Dale, found his tongue.

"Like in a bar. A girl as pretty as you, well, we'd send her a drink. But this," he looked around, "is a waffle house. So, we sent you a side of bacon."

She looked him in the eye. Eyes. They were as brown as hers were blue.

"Give me your hand," she said. She pulled a marker out of her jean pocket and wrote her number on the inside of his wrist.

Marva woke up when her head jerked sideways, a shooting pain down her neck. She thought she was in her studio on campus, Dale's weight pushing her small bones into the cement floor, skin against skin, the sparks of a new love reflected in the windows beside them, but a persistent beeping told her otherwise. The oven timer. Three beeps. Pause. Three beeps. The smoke alarm was silent.

She breathed in the aroma of burnt food. If there was a fire, it was out. The cookies must have turned into chunks of carbon permanently welded to the baking tray. She couldn't feel her legs at all beyond her hip bones. Her tongue kept sticking to her teeth, and her contacts were scratchy. Her little fingers were bruised purple from pounding.

The front of the pie safe stretched out before her like a blank canvas. She stroked it with her index finger, and she imagined the color transferring to the flat surface. Blue for the sky, she painted in broad strokes, then brown for the earth. With just the tip of her finger she painted three golden brown strips that held the sky to the earth like bandages.

Linda H. Heuring

VICTIM OF CIRCUMSTANCE

When Henry Elms saw his wife's photo on the television, the first thing he thought was how she would somehow blame him. Not for the fact that she was missing, although who the Dutch police suspected was a different matter. No, Henry Elms knew she would blame him for allowing the police to broadcast that god-awful passport photo on the St. Maarten Cable.

"So tell me, Henry, didn't you have anything else to give them?" she would say.

"They took my camera and my computer, Hillary. They had plenty to choose from. They chose the passport photo. Something official and all that, I presume. It wasn't my doing," he would say. But even in his imaginary conversation, it sounded like an excuse.

His wife was not a vain woman. A vain woman would have dressed up for an official photo. Hillary squeezed in a 2:00 a.m. stop at the 24-hour grocery store's camera department on her way home from the hospital. A vain woman would have been fuming instead of laughing when the clerk with marginal English couldn't adjust the umbrella lights to accommodate such a tall subject.

"She wouldn't let me help," Hillary had said, dropping the long-shadowed photos on his desk.

"No touch from customer," Hillary said in an accent of undistinguishable origin. Hillary wasn't good with accents. She could read both Spanish and French, but everything out of her mouth sounded like her native Midwestern English.

"She only came up to here," Hillary said, pointing at her lower ribs and laughing.

"You could go back and try again. Reshoot."

"It's just a passport photo. Nobody sees it but some bureaucrats, and I'm sure they've seen worse."

For once Hillary was wrong. It was not only being broadcast on the island of St. Maarten, both the Dutch and the French sides, but Henry figured by now the headline was on the cable news crawls back home. The crawl. That's what they called that annoying bit of business running across the bottom of the screen, distracting you from whatever the one with perfect teeth mouthed with such breathless enthusiasm. "Chicago surgeon missing from Caribbean island resort" would be wedged in between this celebrity's weight loss and that one's gain, moving so slowly across the screen a pre-schooler could sound out the words. Eventually the story would move from the crawl to the feature box with Hillary's passport photo, and Hillary would blame him.

"Really, they didn't let me help," he said aloud.

The police officer on the balcony, Henry forgot his name, interrupted his phone call to glance his way. Henry shook his head. With Hillary's hours and his own inconsistent writing schedule, his voice was the only one he heard most days. Once home, Hillary was likely to be called back or called away. Even on this trip she had scheduled a lecture on bullet wounds, her specialty, as a favor to her former student George Bernard, who now taught here at the American University of the Caribbean School of Medicine.

She certainly got enough practice, with wounds, that is. Schoolchildren were being gunned down in Chicago, victims of drive-bys and turf wars. South Side preachers became statisticians, bellowing from the pulpit what the *Tribune* tallied in print, a running total of public school students shot, killed. Hillary's charge was to save those who could be. Repair the damage to the abdomen of the first-grader hit while walking to school or the shoulder of the gang initiate naive enough to tangle with Chicago's finest. Henry once asked her how she could call the time of death for a victim, especially a child, then turn around and work on the shooter.

"I don't have time to judge. If he's on my table, he's mine to fix," she said. "Besides, most shooters are just kids themselves. Victims, too. Victims of circumstance."

The circumstances were that Hillary did have a touch, an insight into the projectile's path that went beyond just patching up. Victims from three states arrived by helicopter to have her long fingers debride their wounds and coax fragments of metal from muscle and organs slick with blood.

Sometimes in those disorienting hours before dawn when her cell phone vibrated against her water glass on the nightstand, Henry would follow her to the den where she linked by computer to a doctor in San Francisco or Santiago or san-somewhere. Henry would brew the coffee, and Hillary would drink, overlapping her fingers around the mug, focused only on the screen filled with a black and white x-ray or the brilliant colors of a wound lit by a camera in surgery, yellow fat cells, too-white bones, pajama-striped muscles. Henry would settle into his heavy leather chair, out of camera shot, and read, and sometimes shake his head at her pitiful accent, but never doubting her skill. Never doubting her at all.

The phone rang in the condo, and Henry grabbed it, the receiver cheap and insubstantial in his hand. The officer glared and wrapped his hand around Henry's, turning the receiver so they both could hear. His name tag was level with Henry's eyes. Geherty. He must remember to call him that.

"Hello." Henry craned his neck to speak into the handset.

"Dr. Bernard here. Any word?"

Henry shook his head.

"Mr. Elms?"

"Yes, I mean no," Henry said. "Yes, I'm here. No, there's no news, I'm afraid."

"It was only two blocks, you know," Bernard said.

Henry knew how far it was. They had walked it their first night on the island, walked it as far as the front steps, just up a small hill in the road from the condo, left past the gourmet grocery with the chocolate croissants. She promised to pick up croissants on the way back from the lecture. The lecture she didn't give.

"Right," Henry said. "Quite."

Geherty made a cutting motion across his throat.

"Bernard, I must go. Keep the line clear and all that." Henry hung up.

Geherty clamped his hand on Henry's shoulder.

"What did we say about the phone, Mr. Elms?"

"I know, I jumped the gun."

"Let it ring at least twice, then punch the speaker button." Geherty demonstrated. Like kindergarten. A loud dial tone and the button glowed red. Red for danger? For stop?

"I know, Officer Geherty, I know," Henry said.

Geherty opened his cell phone and dialed.

"Just the doctor from the med school," he said. "Roger that." He stashed the phone in a holder on his belt.

"Inspector Wyman is due shortly," he said to Henry.

"He has news?"

"No. Questions."

Henry swallowed. His saliva tasted like metal. The coffee pot was nearly empty. How many pots had he made today? Last night? Countless. He dumped the grounds and rinsed out the carafe. He filled the reservoir with bottled water. He measured coffee with a spoon. When the brew began to hiss and cover the bottom of the carafe, he brought out cheeses and a foil of butter and a stale but edible baguette. He carried a tray to the table on the balcony.

"I had to have something to eat," Henry said. "Help yourself."

Henry spread camembert on a crust of bread. The sea was a shifting palate of greens and blues. Even from their eighth-floor balcony he could see clear to the bottom in the shallows, wavy contours and shadows of sand shifting from movement of the water or creatures unknown. A turtle bigger than a man's head swam a few yards from shore then disappeared. Henry squinted, but it was gone.

Hillary's passport photo was on television again. Her hair was damp from her after-surgery shower. A hint of a line snaked across her forehead from the cap she wore in the operating room, a line that was becoming a permanent wrinkle. Henry had traced that line with his finger many nights as she slept in the crook of his arm. She who learned not to waste a minute of potential sleep by reliving her day snored against the hollow chest of a wide-awake man who was not only reliving the days of his characters, but plotting their next moves.

Henry stretched out his arm and yawned. Had he dozed off? He had been afraid to sleep, fearful that his dreams, such vivid fodder for his books, would play through possible scenarios for Hillary. He made his living with his imagination, after all. He wiped his palm across his face.

Inside, a man in a close-fitting yellow golf shirt and dress slacks ran his hand along the spines of books in the three rows of assorted paperbacks the condo advertisement called a "beach library." Henry had done the same thing when he arrived, finding two of his own titles. The man tipped two books with his fingers and pulled them out. Henry winced to see the top one had no cover.

"Inspector Wyman, Mr. Elms." He shook Henry's hand. "It's a pleasure to meet you, although we could ask for better circumstances." He dropped the books on the table.

"Any news?" Henry said.

"Please, be seated, Mr. Elms."

Geherty picked up the cheese board and the empty coffee cups from the table.

"Any news about my wife?" Henry asked again.

"You need me to stick around, Geert?" Geherty said.

Wyman shook his head. Geherty nodded to Henry and went inside.

"Inspector, what have you learned?" Henry said. He sat forward in his chair.

Wyman looked toward the water.

Henry waited, but he could tell there was no news, good or bad. He sighed. When Geherty closed the front door, Wyman pulled a digital tape recorder from his pocket.

"You don't mind, do you, Mr. Elms?"

Henry shook his head. He sat back. The recording would be worthless out here. The wind, music from the pool bar below, even the waves against the seawall would compete with their voices. No, the tape recorder was a signal to Henry that the search for Hillary had shifted from "she decided not to lecture" to "perhaps she was kidnapped," to the predictable next stage: "it must be the husband." Henry knew the drill. He wrote the drill. Fourteen detective novels dismissed as formula by the critics, designated best sellers by his readers, except for a dud or two. Mr. Elms, indeed. Wyman had nothing, or he would have led with it.

"If you don't mind, Mr. Elms, let's backtrack a bit. Whose idea was this holiday?"

"If her body would cooperate, Inspector, my wife would never leave the operating room."

"So it was your idea."

Henry nodded. He and Hillary had argued about the dates.

"It's not a good time, Henry. Things pick up when school starts," she said.

"In the spring you say things pick up in the summer, Hil, and we both know about the holidays. What do you think, everyone will wake up one morning and call a cease-fire so you can go on vacation?"

Hillary gave him that look, that slightly exasperated look, and wiped her bangs off her forehead with her left pinky, as if brushing away her thoughts. She closed her eyes, inhaled, then exhaled slowly.

"Make sure I have internet access," she said. Then she smiled. "And a beach."

"What's that, Mr. Elms?" Wyman said.

"A beach," Henry said. "She wanted a beach."

"And you, Mr. Elms? What did you want?"

A fresh start, Henry thought. Get out of that grimy city, somewhere people didn't honk their horns every time a traffic light changed, where the words could flow through his fingers with heat and passion, instead of the bitter frozen lexis he'd created in the last year.

"I wanted to see Hillary in a bathing suit again." Henry chuckled in what he hoped was a manly way. "No room for a pager in a bikini."

Wyman didn't speak.

"I wanted to spend time with my wife," Henry said. "Get her out of the hospital, out of the city." He knew Wyman's silence was meant to prod him to chatter away, yet knowing it and controlling himself were two different things. Henry put his hands in his lap and pinched the skin inside his thumb. If only he weren't so tired.

"You don't spend time together in Chicago?"

"Of course we do. But we're both working. On holiday we don't have other obligations."

"Although Dr. Elms was to give a lecture, and you, Mr. Elms, brought your laptop."

"You know the lecture was a favor," Henry said. He was getting a little hot now. "We both use the laptop for internet access. And a writer is never really on vacation, you know. You have to be prepared to take dictation from your muse."

"Your muse, it appears, has been in hibernation." Wyman picked up one of the paperbacks: *Low Down Under*. "This came out four years ago," Wyman said. "Then three years ago, this one you called *Pheasant Under Glass*." He fingered the rough edge where the cover had been torn off. "No cover means this book was sent back because it didn't sell. Remanded, isn't that what you call it?"

"Remanded is your word, Inspector. For books it's 'remaindered.'"

Wyman waved his hand from the wrist. "No matter. Your books are no longer selling."

Henry felt his face turning red.

"That particular book was not my best. My others continue to sell quite steadily."

"But you haven't written anything in the last three years."

"Published. I have written." Hell, yes, he had written. He had written every day, hundreds, thousands of words, racing across the screen as fast as he could type, only to find the stories themselves disappearing, one after another leaping to their deaths like suicidal lemmings. Actually, mass suicide of lemmings was a myth, Henry learned. They were more likely to turn on each other in times of overcrowding or stress, but that didn't fit the simile. And Henry loved a good simile.

"As I understand it, you owe your publisher a book."

Henry frowned. Who had he been talking to? His agent? How did he get through? Henry himself hadn't been able to get Sidney on the line in months. "When you have something for me, I'll talk to you," Sidney told him back in January. Now when he called he got only Sidney's assistant, who always asked if there was a draft yet.

"How did you meet your wife?" Wyman said.

Henry scraped his chair on the floor and stood. "Is this relevant?" He shook his left leg, which had gone to sleep.

"Everything is relevant, Mr. Elms."

"I met her at a book signing," Henry said. She came in late to his reading, striking in green scrubs with a red backpack. The book she brought for signing was cluttered with sticky notes and awash in pink highlighter.

"I'm a surgery resident," she told him, tossing her ponytail over her shoulder.

"I love your books," she said. Henry was mesmerized. Her fingers were so long they nearly wrapped around the book, and they were slender, with the cleanest short nails he'd ever seen.

She hesitated. She took in a breath as if getting up her courage, then called his description of gunshot wounds "literary bunk." She had the pages marked, and she was so earnest, so sure he wanted things to be exactly accurate, he had no chance to be insulted. That was twelve years and eight books ago.

"And her parents disapproved of you?"

Sid and Hil's parents? He's certainly been burning up the phone lines, Henry thought.

"At first," Henry said. Hillary's father, so smug in his library filled with books collected rather than read, had made his position quite clear. Henry's profession, particularly in that low-brow genre, and Henry's physical attributes, dark, soft and a little on the pudgy side he had to admit, were just not of Hillary's caliber. Had he really said "caliber," or was Henry projecting? Wouldn't Henry do "what was best for Hillary" and kindly disappear? They married six weeks later.

"And now?" Wyman said.

"They've mellowed, but we don't see them." Henry leaned on the balcony rail.

Wyman pulled out his phone and tapped the screen.

"So, you didn't have dinner with them on the 19th?"

"Absolutely not."

"Would it surprise you that your wife did?"

"I'm surprised she didn't mention it," Henry said. Wyman stared at him, and Henry knew he was looking for tells. Body language. Hesitation. How many times he had written this same scene over coffee, a beer, in glass-walled interrogation rooms? Henry could never remember if studies showed liars looked to the left or to the right. He always had to look that up.

Wyman consulted his phone.

"'Agitated' is what her mother called her. 'Like she was afraid of something.' Any idea what she might have been afraid of, Mr. Elms?"

Henry had seen Hillary afraid only once, when he was writing *Take a Bullet* and had dragged her with him to an outdoor demonstration on bullet-resistant windows. A bullet ricocheted off the target and whizzed by her ear. She sat in the car for the rest of the demonstration. Henry thought she might throw up.

"Just like that," she said on the drive home. "Only a few seconds and my life is over."

Henry knew she didn't mean her living, breathing life, but her life as a surgeon, the only thing that mattered to her besides Henry. Later, the company sent her a paperweight, a square of polycarbonate with a bullet imbedded in it. She could rub her finger over the "wound" and touch the metal bullet. The back of the block bulged out, but the bullet hadn't made it through. Henry had no idea why she kept it around. And no idea anything was bothering her.

"I'm not sure her mother is the best judge," Henry said.

"Strange, she said the same thing about you."

"Meaning?" Henry leaned over the table. "Are you even looking for my wife, Inspector? I'm no stranger to police work. I know the process. At a minimum, tell me what you're doing to find her or release me from this trumped up house arrest so I can look myself."

"The process, as you call it, may be quite different here than in America. I can assure you we are leaving no stone unturned." Wyman smiled. *Stone Unturned* was Henry's breakout novel.

"Have a seat, Mr. Elms." Wyman smiled again, and

Henry wanted to slap that sneer off his face, but instead turned away.

Two sunset booze cruise catamarans idled just offshore. Tourists waved. Someone switched on the lights at the pool bar. Soon the sun would find the horizon, and the pool's underwater lights would send a blue-green glow up to Henry's balcony to usher in the night. A second night without Hillary.

"Your wife is quite a wealthy woman, Mr. Elms. Was there a prenuptial agreement?"

"No," Henry shook his head. "We never felt the need. We both brought a lot to the table."

"And your side of the table? How does that look these days?"

"My investments were hit like anyone else's."

"But not Dr. Elm's investments."

"Her father is a financial planner. He manages her portfolio."

"But not yours."

"By mutual agreement. What's your point?"

"Let me lay it out for you, Mr. Elms. A rich and beautiful woman falls for a best-selling author who after a few years isn't so successful. Perhaps he lost his charm or grew a paunch."

Henry looked down in spite of himself.

"Perhaps she sees her parents were right after all and wants out. She finds more in common with another doctor. Closer in age. Her professional equal."

Henry felt a twinge. Once Hillary was too tired to drive home, and he insisted on picking her up, taking her out for breakfast. He pulled under the hospital entrance canopy to see Hillary embracing a tall man in scrubs. In the car, her eyes were dark, as if she'd deliberately pulled down a shade.

"Tough night?" Henry had said, trying to lift her mood. "You'll feel better after we get a little food in you."

"My cases aren't make-believe, Henry," she said. "A pregnant fifteen-year-old was shot by a jealous wife. Gut shot. The baby was full of holes. I spent six solid hours on the mother before I lost her, too. I can't finish the chapter and order some French toast."

Wyman was still theorizing.

"The writer, accustomed to the finer things, won't give her up. He takes her on a trip, a last ditch effort to patch things up. When that, too, fails, she conveniently disappears. Murdered for her money."

Henry was expecting the accusation, but still it gave him chills. His skin itched. Over the past few months he had examined their marriage without blinders, or so he thought, and pronounced it sound, playing scenes in his mind as if he had written them, testing them for truth, authenticity. Had his marriage, like his words, betrayed him and rushed headlong into death?

It was dark now. The green and yellow control lights on the hot tub gave Wyman's face a ghoulish cast. Henry had nothing to say.

A woman's scream stopped the band downstairs. The bartender and a security guard rushed to where she was pointing—the steps from the beach. Hillary, barefoot and soaking wet, staggered up onto the patio.

A half-hour later, Hillary's clothes were in an evidence bag, and beneath her robe, her legs were scratched and dotted with bug bites. She refused a rape examination, and she flat out wouldn't talk until she'd showered.

"I may have been raped professionally, but certainly not physically," she told Wyman in her surgeon's voice. "Don't you think I'd be the first to know?"

Wyman open his mouth as if to protest, then sat down. It was Henry's turn to smile. Wyman led Hillary through the past two days, prodding her to remember faces, landmarks.

Henry sat next to her on the blue-cushioned wicker couch and held her hand when she wasn't waving it about. She described the scrubby island, the tin shack, the generator out back, and the antibiotics and sterile surgery kit they'd produced from thin air.

"They're resourceful," Wyman said. "They nabbed a crack surgeon."

"He was lucky," Hillary said. "Against my orders, they moved him tonight."

Henry could see her in the shack, surrounded by men with automatics, bare bulb swinging, barking geckos near the ceiling. Hillary putting her foot down, in her halting Spanish, of course. A surgeon first, then a woman, but never a victim.

They'd dumped her overboard a couple hundred yards from the beach, his Viola, cast into the sea but served up safely on shore. Henry saw a few grains of sand glisten at her hairline. Damp curls hugged her temple. Viola coughed up seawater and wiped her mouth on the back of her hand. The hands that had been forced to save the life of the leader of the revolution.

Henry stroked Hillary's hand and saw slim fingers caress a Walther PPK. No, not a PPK, a Beretta 90two with a custom grip. If Viola hadn't left the gun in the condo, she'd never have been kidnapped at all. She had taken an oath to do no harm, but that didn't make her a fool. "Do No Harm" might work, he thought, or maybe "Oath of Harm." Viola changed into black skinny jeans and holstered the Beretta over a black T-shirt. She ran her fingers through her hair and felt the knot where she'd been thumped two days ago. She was going back out there. This time on her terms.

Henry hadn't slept in two days, but he was wide awake, his synapses firing, his fingers in need of a keyboard.

"I am in dire need of a nightcap and a few hours between some clean sheets," Hillary said. She stood up. Henry, too.

"My computer," he said to Wyman. "I need my computer."

"You can pick it up in the morning," Wyman said.

"No, I need it now. Tonight," Henry said. He would never be able to get this on paper fast enough longhand. Viola might run away, follow the others off the cliff. He didn't even know if they had blank paper to get started.

"You took it, I'd suggest you return it," Hillary said, "within the hour."

She smoothed the collar on Henry's polo shirt.

"What you may not understand, Inspector, is that if his body would cooperate, my husband wouldn't leave his desk at all when his muse is visiting."

Henry opened and closed the drawers in the living room, shuffling through card decks and games and wayward knobs and screws, looking for paper. Hillary poured two glasses of Courvoisier and sorted through the papers on the coffee table. She held up the island newspaper with two fingers while she sipped.

"Oh, Henry," she said, turning the front page toward him. "How could you let them use that photo? Didn't you have anything else to give them?"

WHATEVER WILL DO

The ink was barely dry on Frank Cowan's will when Ebenezer reviewed the estate with Cowan's grieving daughter. It was a simple will for a man with few assets. That was a good thing, because Ebenezer had a plane to catch.

If only he could get Edith Cowan out of his office.

"So, that's it, is it?" she asked again. She was planted on the couch, the austerity of her black suit offset by a red silk scarf. Ebenezer preferred to read wills from the seating area near the window instead of across his desk. It just wouldn't do to have all that wood between himself and the grieving family. No, it was too cold. It just wouldn't do.

"If there's nothing else," Ebenezer brushed his hands across the knees of his pants, grabbing a quick, and he hoped, discrete, look at his watch. Ten-thirty. He knew he should have scheduled this reading earlier, but Cowan's daughter couldn't get there sooner.

Edith Cowan sighed, a deep, sad sound that could

signal she was getting up, a preparatory exhalation for strength to heave her bulk from the leather cushions, but she only stretched out her legs and crossed her ankles. Her black shoes had straps that circled her ankles like a man's fingers. Ebenezer wondered how much of his hand it would take to reach around. Could he use his index finger or would he need the extra length of his middle finger? She had ankles, Edith Cowan did. Ankles, indeed.

"My father," Edith began.

Ebenezer quickly folded his hands, startled. He smiled and nodded for her to continue.

"My father thought a lot of you," she said, leaning forward and looking him straight in the eyes. "'He's rock solid,' my father used to say. 'You'll have to meet him. A man of substance. A substantial man.'"

Ebenezer blushed. In other cultures a big man was to be respected. Weight was a sign of prosperity. Not here. A big man was more than likely to be pitied, if he was an aging athlete, or scorned, if he wasn't. Frank Cowan had been a small man himself, built like a jockey with ears like Ross Perot. Ordinarily Ebenezer would feel clumsy and awkward around such a diminutive man, especially one who sized him up every time with those darting measuring eyes. Then again, it was always business. First, Ebenezer was the customer, standing in front of a three-way mirror at Zaxby's Tailors, as Cowan walked around him with a yellow tailor's tape. Later, it was Cowan who sat across Ebenezer's walnut desk, signing the papers for his last will and testament.

"Your father was a gentleman. He will be missed," Ebenezer said. He reached across the coffee table for Edith's copy of the will and slipped it into a navy blue envelope with a string-tie clasp.

"If there's nothing else," he said, again, holding the

envelope toward her. He couldn't stand before a lady stood. It just wouldn't do.

"I'm sorry," she said, and without warning she was upright with her pocketbook in one hand, her other hand outstretched to shake. "You must have other appointments."

Ebenezer shook her hand, his face solemn. "Actually," he said, "I do have a plane to catch."

The plane ticket, and the stay at an all-inclusive resort just south of Cancun was, ironically, a prize from Zaxby's in a drawing Ebenezer didn't remember entering.

"It was just for our plus-size customers," Cowan had told him, handing over a packet of information on the resort and a plane ticket. "Your name was chosen. The resort, it is built with you in mind."

"It's not going to be full of attorneys, is it?" Ebenezer made one of his rare jokes, he was so shocked at winning such an expensive prize.

"It should fit like the perfect pair of pants," Cowan had said. Two weeks later the little tailor was dead.

∞

Ebenezer hadn't had his shirt off in public since elementary school. He hadn't worn shorts outside his house since junior high. Yet here he was, stretched out on a beach chair between the pool and the turquoise blue water of the Caribbean Sea, dressed in a bathing suit of a color and pattern he wouldn't have dreamed he would buy, let alone wear. His flawless white skin reflected the orange and yellow of the tropical print, as if a blooming dandelion had been gently rubbed just above the elastic of his trunks and left its yellow promise of love behind.

"No Fear" stickers were plastered on the cash register

at the gift shop, a brand of beach gear, the clerk told him. And fear was what he left behind the minute he walked into the lobby at the resort. Everything was built to eliminate risk for the above-average-sized traveler. Chairs were wider. Beds were big and sturdy. Showers were spacious, and even the beach chairs were made of metal, wide enough to stretch out without hanging over, with blue cushions as thick as on his couch at home. In the dining room there were no booths, only sturdy tables with starched cloths. The waiters brought a selection of foods, and plenty of them, without once turning up their noses at his choice of food or quantity. A man could eat here, Ebenezer thought. He could indeed.

"You need lotion?"

Ebenezer lifted a crooked elbow to look directly at the neck of a Mexican woman in a yellow hotel smock. She couldn't have been more than four feet tall.

"You need lotion?" she repeated, holding a bottle of sunscreen by the lid and pointing at Ebenezer's acre of white back above his trunks. In her other hand she held a red wooden stool, its seat laced with some kind of a reed or cane or woven palm frond. Ebenezer wasn't up on his tropical vegetation.

"*Si*," he replied, trying out his Spanish. He could count to ten and say yes, no, and thanks. "*Gracias*," he added.

She tamped the stool's legs into the sand and climbed on. Ebenezer rested his head on his chin, closing his eyes as the woman's strong hands spread the warm lotion across his shoulders, then down his back, massaging the lotion into his skin, first in strokes so long her shift dragged across his back, then in short, circular motions, wax on, wax off. He tried to think of something other than her hands on his skin. He opened his eyes, scouring the sand near his chair for a crab, a bit of seaweed, anything to distract him, when ten toes with bright red nails stopped directly in front of him. The toes were poking out of a pair of jute espadrilles with braided straps crossing and circling a pair of ankles that made him catch his breath.

The lotion lady stopped abruptly. "*Lo siento*," she said. "*Lo siento.*"

She stepped down from her stool and backed away. "*Lo siento*," she said again.

"I don't know what you are saying," Ebenezer said. "What happened? What did I do?" He started to rise, to turn over, but the lotion lady was gone. He sat on the edge of his chair, and the ankles that had taken his breath away were now crossed in front of him. They were attached to a woman covered by a bright blue beach robe and matching hat with oversized sunglasses who now parked on the chair next to him.

"I'm sorry," the lady in blue said.

"Pardon me," Ebenezer said before he really listened. "Oh," he added as he realized what she had said. "For what?"

"No, not me. Her," she pointed to the lotion lady who was now greasing up another guest. "She said she was sorry. *Lo siento.* That's what it means. Well, literally it means 'I feel it,' sort of like 'I feel your pain.' I'm sorry."

Ebenezer rubbed his hand across his chin and his arm brushed up against his own breast. He realized he was uncovered and grabbed for his towel. "How did you say that? Los iendo?"

"Low-sea-IN-tow," she said slowly. "For what?"

"I usually stay covered up in public," he said.

The woman pulled her robe apart like the warm up silk of a boxer in the ring and let it drop to her feet in the sand. She stepped over it and brought her ankles together on the lounger.

"Don't cover up on my account," she said, like she meant it.

Ebenezer let his towel slowly slide back down. So was this what other men did at the beach? He reached out a hand.

"Ebenezer. Ebenezer Lassiter," he said.

The woman grasped his fingers. "Don't tell me I'm THAT forgettable," she said.

Ebenezer looked at her again. Did he meet her on the shuttle to the hotel? Did she work there? Did he sit near her at breakfast?

"You'll have to forgive me," he began.

"In your office. Yesterday?" she said.

Oh, God, he realized it was the Cowan woman. Edith. Ebenezer grabbed his towel again, yanking it up to his shoulders like a junior high girl surprised in a locker room.

"Sorry, Miss Cowan. Truly sorry, I didn't recognize you." He fumbled for his shirt. A mistake, a rotten mistake to lay out here half naked, even if he was thousands of miles from home. This just wouldn't do. No, not at all. As he clutched the towel, Edith Cowan bent over, digging for something in her beach bag.

"It's *lo siento*, remember? You'll get the hang of it before the week's out," she said without looking at him.

He stuffed his feet into his beach shoes, preparing to excuse himself, to stand up and race to his room where he would what, pack? Collapse in a mound on the tile floor? Stand in an icy cold shower? The water wasn't that cold here, though. Room temperature was more like 80 degrees. A tepid shower?

"Finally," she said. Ebenezer clamped his sunglasses down over his eyes and peered at her. She was holding a bottle of lotion out like a flask of bourbon. "Since you scared off the lotion lady, be a dear, will you, and put some of this on my back? You do me, then I'll do you."

Ebenezer coughed and yanked at his shirt that was half on and half off, caught on his left elbow like a kite in a bare oak. "Las shinko," he mumbled, ducking his head and holding his shirt closed. He shuffled off, failing to control the unfamiliar sandals, which made decided flips to the sides just as his heels flopped toward the sand.

Once inside his beachfront room, Ebenezer slid his fingers between the frame of the patio door and the curtain and gently spread the gap to home in on Edith Cowan. She was on her stomach with the back of her bathing suit undone. The lotion lady was on the stool beside her. The lotion lady leaned over Edith, her hands dark and quick against Edith's fairness. Ebenezer could feel those hands on him, too, and he imagined his hands on Edith's back, on her breasts that were flattened against the blue padding of the chair, ample pools spreading out to the side where her loosened suit fell away. The curtain quivered as his hand shook. The lotion lady stepped down from her stool, and Edith raised up, her suit barely askew, but askew none-the-less, held up with one hand while she rummaged in the bag. She placed something in the lotion lady's hand. A tip, of course, Ebenezer thought. The lady backed away, and Edith smiled toward Ebenezer's patio door. He stepped back, as if she could really see inside.

Ebenezer breathed in ten times quickly, and it made him dizzy. Thinking about a client this way was a breach of his ethics, his personal ethics, not some state bar-regulated behavior code. It just wouldn't do to have a relationship with her. Not that he'd had other personal relationships with women. Surely she would understand. He stripped off his bathing suit and shirt and stepped into the coolness of the tile shower. There was no door, just strategically placed blocks to keep the water contained. He turned and stretched out his arms, something he couldn't do in the cramped tub-shower in his apartment back home. Ebenezer closed his eyes and let the warm water paint him with grace, a lightness to his limbs he had only experienced while asleep, and only remembered for a few precious minutes after awakening, before his dreams were accosted by reality and staggered off in defeat. He moved from under the spray to soap up, when he heard a pounding on his door. Housekeeping? He wasn't expecting anyone.

He opened the door in his bathrobe, a good bit of water making its way down his legs into a puddle on the floor. He was prepared for housekeeping, but not for Edith Cowan.

"Can I come in?" Her sentence may have lilted upward at the end, like a question, but there was no question she was coming right on in. "Looks a lot like my room, only neater," she joked, glancing at the bathing suit and shirt dropped on the floor. Ebenezer bent to pick them up, and Edith balanced herself on the edge of the bed.

"I . . ." Ebenezer's face was red from bending over, from Edith's forwardness, from embarrassment at being seen in his bathrobe.

"Look, before you get bent out of shape," Edith interrupted.

"Wait," Ebenezer said in a rush. If he didn't hurry, he was afraid he wouldn't get the words out. "I need you to know that it is against my code of ethics to have any kind of a non-professional relationship with a client. It just won't do."

"What client?" Edith asked.

"Why, you," he stammered.

"My father was your client," she said. "I'm just, well, I don't know what that makes me, but I'm definitely not your client. You see, I'm not planning to pay you for anything."

Edith lifted one leg and touched the hem of Ebenezer's robe. Her ankle bones were more prominent when she pointed her toes. Ebenezer thought of a ballerina.

"Did my father ever talk about my mother?" Edith asked. She flexed her foot and Ebenezer felt the breeze as his robe fluttered. He could step back, but he was frozen to the spot, his eyes fixed to her leg. He rubbed his tongue around inside his mouth, hoping for some moisture to allow him to speak.

"Only that she had passed," he said finally.

"The love of his life," Edith sighed. She riffled in her bag again and stood next to Ebenezer and held up a photo from her wallet. They were standing beside a palm tree, and if Frank Cowan hadn't had a full head of hair in the photo, Ebenezer would have sworn Cowan was standing at this very resort beside Edith.

"You favor her," Ebenezer said.

"He had a sense about people," Edith said, moving to the patio door and peeking out as Ebenezer did before. "Uncanny, really. Like he knew what they needed before they did."

It was Ebenezer's turn to sit on the bed. He pulled his bathrobe tight. He was dry now. The water by the door had almost evaporated. From the beginning Cowan had inspired Ebenezer's trust, like he had his best interest in mind. Ebenezer was more than a body to be dressed; he was a man of substance.

"Like us, for instance," she said, turning to face Ebenezer, "and this trip."

It began to dawn on Ebenezer that he had been set up, tossed onto the beach with Edith by her dying father, his favorite tailor, the man who knew his body as well as anyone.

He waited for the anger, that familiar rise in blood pressure that had come to his defense since third grade when he was forced into a janitor's closet with the class fat girl. Paired off. Humiliated. But it wasn't his blood pressure that rose. There was instead a swelling in his throat and a blurring of his eyes that he fought to control. He turned his head to the wall and wiped his nose on his sleeve. At his feet Edith's beach robe formed a soft pedestal on the floor, her bare legs rising like a Yule marble goddess from the blue depths of a cenote. He felt the bed shift ever so slightly as she sat beside him. Her hand was cool and smooth on his bare neck.

Ebenezer slid his hands down to the ties of his bathrobe. He could pull them tighter, jump up, and send her away. He could politely stand and ask her to leave. He could do any number of things, but what he couldn't do was turn her away. That just wouldn't do.

ONE CHAIR AWAY

If it's news to you that Roy owned the only drive-thru funeral parlor in Maine, you've never been to the Capri Towers at Clearwater Beach or your hearing aid needs new batteries. You don't have to waste any breath asking what he did in his old life, B.R., before retirement. He just blurts it out, strutting around by the pool in his bathing suit and that ridiculous hat with the flamingos hanging down where ear flaps would be if you lived up North. Most all of us have come from up North somewhere, but I thought people from the East always booked it down I-95 to Lauderdale or West Palm or Miami, leaving the Gulf Coast to us Midwesterners. It's not the first time I've been wrong.

Roy wasn't bad looking in a pasty newcomer kind of way. His legs were pale as peppermint sticks, but his chest wasn't too gray-hairy, and he had just the smallest of paunches, more like a volleyball behind his navel. Not one of those spare tires that hangs over the elastic like some I could point out. Ike, for one, who carries that portable bar in a leather case downstairs every morning and sets it up on one of the tables under the portico and makes Mojitos or gin and something drinks, all of them shaken, not stirred, and his belly jiggles coming and going. One of these days one side is going to meet the other coming back around, and the man will knock himself out. There's a doctor or two here, but they're so far past retired, I don't know that I'd let them take my temperature, let alone give me CPR. That doesn't mean I wouldn't fetch one to help out poor Ike if push came to shove.

Roy pulled up a chair at the table where Ike was grinding mint leaves in the bottom of a plastic glass, the kind that has little cloth patches in between the layers. You have to use plastic here at the pool or the kids who patrol for the owner's association will give you a warning.

"Now, Mrs. Martin," they say, like I'm in kindergarten, "you don't want anyone cutting their feet on broken glass now, do you?"

Who do they think made up rules about glass anyway? We parents, now grandparents, or worse. Besides, it's "his or her" feet, not "their." I didn't teach English for twenty-seven years to hear bad grammar.

"You ever been through a drive-thru at a funeral home?" Roy said.

Ike ground away. I could smell the mint from my lounge chair. I always sat one lounger away from the portico. Close enough to hear, far enough away to ignore them if I wanted.

"Can't say I have," Ike said. "Mojito?" He held the glass up toward Roy.

"Don't mind if I do," Roy said. He ran a palm down his chest like he was smoothing his tie. "I had the only drive-thru funeral business in Maine," he said. "Nothing like it.

I got an award for the design. Even gave a talk on it at the NFDA convention in Chicago in '07."

"What do the Mexicans have to do with the funeral business?" Ike said. His belly was rolling with the shaker now. He could power a small city if you hooked him up with a hula hoop. "I haven't heard one good thing come out of that agreement."

"N-F-D-A," Roy said, with emphasis on the D. "National Funeral Director's Association. Not NAFTA."

Ike covered the leaves with liquid and floated an intact leaf on top. He handed the glass to Roy.

"I'd be steering clear of there myself," Ike said. "Never had much use for Chicago. 'Course I've never been there, but my cousin Frank once got lost going through there on his way to see Mt. Rushmore, and he told me the roads were more confusing than the instructions for my iPhone. I had to get my grandbaby to set it up for me. Put all the numbers in for speedy dialing. She types with her thumbs."

Any minute now Ike would pull out his iPhone. That phone attracted geezers like a Denny's breakfast special. It could draw a crowd almost as quick as the cherry picker they brought in to clean the windows. Almost. Invariably one guy would say something about Apple stock. Someone would say how long his son-in-law stood in line to buy one, and they'd all shake their heads. Just touching it gave them bragging rights.

I know this because I spend every afternoon down here by the pool, and after a lifetime of studying men, I know a thing or two about their behavior. Jane Goodall has nothing on me. This time of day it's just the men and me and the visitors: kids and grandkids who kill two birds with one stone, checking up on the old folks and getting free room and board on the beach for a week. When the sun moves over the east side of the building and heads toward the Gulf, the other women are upstairs in the AC, taking their siestas and digesting their doggy-bag lunches from last night's early bird specials. It's not that I don't appreciate the other women. Lord knows I could use the company. Just not the competition. There's ten of us for every eight old men, and that includes the married ones. I'm just narrowing the odds.

I opened my beach bag and pulled out a thermos of water and my latest hardback thriller. I always sprang for the hardbacks. One whole wall of my condo is a bookshelf. More than one relationship has begun over sharing my library. I poured a cup of water and drank, checking out the pool deck over the cup's rim. Not many guys out today.

Without looking I could tell Ike pulled out his phone. I heard the scrape of plastic on concrete as Stan and his sister Bambi's widower, Bernie, tossed in their cards and headed over to Ike's makeshift bar. Bambi was her real name—I checked. A little too Disney for me. They had side-by-side condos until their wives died. Now they live in one, I think it was originally Stan's, and rent out the other. Stan had a Velcro pouch hanging from his walker where he kept his Sudoku book and a retractable pencil with a big eraser. He was an actuary from Dayton who wore what appeared to be the same shirt every day. Bernie was the clothes hound. He had a Hooters sleeveless T and a Tommy Bahama knockoff with palm fronds he wore on alternating days. Today was a Hooters day. They acted like an old married couple, bickering over the rules of gin or the details of something way in the past. I had dinner with them one night, and they took so long arguing over the check I almost nodded off at the table.

One of the kids came out of the recreation room and joined the group around Ike. Ike handed him the phone, and the kid held it in his palm like he was filming a TV commercial and showed the guys how to get on the internet.

"Pull up Apple's stock," Stan said.

"He took a big bite of Apple," Bernie said. Always the card, that Bernie.

The kid ran his pointing finger over the screen.

Ike put a handful of mint leaves in another glass and ground away.

"You know mint leaves are good for the digestion," Roy said. "Not to mention the breath."

"You get a discount on breath mints?" Stan said. "At the funeral home?"

Roy smoothed his imaginary tie. "Just whatever Costco gives its members," Roy said. "We do, I mean, we did, go through a lot of them in the summer. Seems like the heat gets to people up there instead of the cold."

"I'd think you'd get a lot of bodies during those primaries with all those people coming into town and trying to influence you," Ike said. "People can't handle the stress."

"That's New Hampshire. I'm from Maine."

"Same difference," Ike shrugged. "One of those little states way up there."

Ike was from Michigan, which to me, being from Kentucky, was "way up there" itself.

"Can you get a map on that thing?" Roy asked the kid who was still holding the phone.

"Sure thing," the kid said. He turned the phone sideways and stretched his fingers out to make the U.S. bigger.

"Mojito?" Ike said.

Roy traded in his glass for a fresh one, discretely pulling a half-chewed mint leaf out of his mouth and dropping it into the dregs.

The kid showed the map to Ike, who shook his head.

"These kids, they can do anything electronic," Ike said. "I had to get my grandbaby to set this up for me. You got any grandbabies, Roy?"

"Two," he said. "My son Roy and his wife have a boy and a girl."

"Roy, Jr. is it?" Bernie said. He stretched out his legs. I could see the thin red line where the doctor had stripped out his long vein to patch up his heart. "I always wanted to name my boy junior, but Bambi wouldn't have anything to do with it."

Roy took a long drink of his Mojito. "Actually, my dad is Jr. My grandfather started the funeral home, and then my dad took over. I'm Roy the third. They used to call me Trey, like three."

"*Uno, dos, tres,*" Ike said.

"So your boy's the fourth?" Stan said.

"*Quattro,*" Ike said. "The baby must be *cinco.*"

Roy adjusted his hat and looked out over the ocean. "No," he said. "They named him Carson, after his wife's father."

A colony of seagulls surrounded a little girl on the beach who held a bag of microwave popcorn. She clutched the bag to her chest, crying. A woman, probably her mother, flapped a beach towel at them. The men just sat and watched until Stan clamped his hands on his walker and pushed himself upright.

"If you'll excuse me," he said. He headed toward the back doors to the restrooms.

"I'll get the door for you, Mr. Levine," the kid said. He gave the phone back to Ike.

"Is he running the shop for you now?" Bernie said. Stan shot him a look over his shoulder as he lurched toward the door.

"No," Roy said. He rattled the ice in his glass. "I sold it."

Bernie wiggled his foot around to find the toe pole on his flip flops and made his way back to the card table. He shuffled and dealt a game of solitaire.

Roy drained his glass and set it on the table for Ike.

"What's the damage here, Ike?" he said.

Ike waved him away. "I do this for fun," Ike said. "You can spring for a bottle sometime. Plastic. "

Roy hiked up his suit and smoothed his chest hair and turned toward the sea.

"This seat taken?" He pointed to the one between me and the portico.

"Help yourself," I said.

He settled into the chair and picked up my book.

"Is this good? I saw it in the bookstore yesterday."

"I just started it last night," I said. I pulled my sunglasses down lower on my nose so he could see my eyes. "You can borrow it when I'm done," I said. "I have a pretty big library, and I like lending books."

Roy nodded.

A nurse in a flowered top came butt first out of the recreation room, pulling Edna in her wheelchair. Edna came out every day about an hour before sunset to get a little air, even when it was so thick you felt like spooning it into your lungs. She and her husband used to walk the beach in the evening until her last stroke. He'd push her around the grounds in her wheelchair of an evening until that night he died in his sleep. Edna had thrown everything on her night stand at the wall to get someone's attention. Now she wore one of those panic buttons on a chain around her neck.

The nurse paused near my chair. Edna's head listed to one side. "Did you hear about Mrs. Schottenstein in 312?"

I shook my head. Mrs. Schottenstein was one of the early birds who scoured the beach for shells every morning.

"Heart attack," she said. "You didn't see the ambulance this morning?"

I shook my head again. I try not to see the ambulances. When I see someone carried out on one of those gurneys, something sinks inside me, like being on a plane when there's turbulence. My body goes one way, but my insides go another. I saw Ike busy himself with the ice bucket. Roy just looked out at the water. The nurse pushed Edna over to the railing that separated the pool from the beach.

A bit of a breeze sent a whiff of gardenias our way. The walk was lined with miniature plants. They were loaded with heavy white blooms against slick dark leaves.

I inhaled and sighed. "I just love gardenias, don't you?"

"They don't grow up where I'm from, but once in a while the florist would send over an arrangement," Roy said.

"Mostly I think of mums and carnations at funerals," I said. "And those big tall gladiolas."

"You know my son hates flowers," he said. "I think that's one reason he left."

"Oh," I said. I pulled my beach towel over my legs.

"In kindergarten his class took a field trip to the arboretum, and they called us to come and get him because he wouldn't stop crying."

"What was wrong?"

"He wouldn't tell his teacher, but when I got there he grabbed my legs and wouldn't let go. He just kept sobbing, 'I smell dead people.' I can still hear him. 'I smell dead people.'"

The sun was orange as it made its way down. It usually was. And it was huge. Further down the beach, at what used to be the Holiday Inn, the same kid sang and played Jimmy Buffet songs every afternoon, and he always played his last one just as the sun disappeared beneath the horizon. I am never ready for the end. It seems like the sun just hangs there in the blue like a kid on the high dive getting up her nerve to jump. But once the lower edge touches the water, it speeds up, melts into a thin orange line across the horizon and disappears.

The sky and the sea were the same darkening blue. Roy turned sideways in his chair and looked at me. "Would you like to get some dinner?" he said.

I put my hand on his arm. "I'd love to."

Roy helped me up. My legs were stiff after sitting so long. I was still getting used to my new hip. A crowd had gathered to watch the sunset, and we walked past the gauntlet of canes and walkers and wheelchairs, all facing east now, headed like moths to the lights of the building.

Roy and I walked the stone bridge in the lobby that stretched over the koi pond with its floating lilies. A tree frog croaked somewhere close, and the air was rich with the perfume of blooming tropical plants. In the colored lights of the rocky waterfall, I saw Roy the fourth, his dad in miniature, wiping his eyes with his fists below a pale high forehead.

"I smell dead people," he said.

Not just yet, Fourth, I told him. Not just yet.

THREE OF THEM

"I got some fudge"

She stops stirring the goat cheese dip she's making for the party and looks up at the old man.

"I got some fudge," he repeats, and he winks at her. There's fudge in his mouth and another piece in his hand. Winks, like she'll think it's cute that he took food off the party tray in the dining room a half hour before the guests arrive. Years ago, when it wasn't her party tray or her house, but the house of maybe his first wife, she might have joined him in a wink, or at least smiled when the wife ranted at him for snacking from the wrong tray. When did that change? When he no longer had a wife and started in on her instead?

His stair-chair squeaks then whirs to life. Two beeps. It's moving. He's headed back upstairs.

She checks the dessert plate in the dining room. There are no empty spaces. He took some and rearranged all the pieces so she can't tell. He's had to touch several others to do that. Maybe all of them. Does he do it on purpose?

"Look, I'm old but I've still got it. I can drive a woman mad." What is he thinking? Or does he think at all?

She doesn't like him touching her food because he won't wash his hands. Or, if he does, afterwards he sticks his fingers way inside his ears and roots around or blows his nose and then doesn't wash again. Touching her food.

"Howard Hughes," she tells her husband. "I'm turning into Howard Hughes, and I hate it. His idiosyncrasies without his money."

"I never eat sweets," the old man has said for years, a family joke when he lives somewhere else. A different matter when he lives in your house. Especially when it's Christmas.

In two days he eats all the Christmas fudge, what was in the pan ready to replenish the party tray, what she pulled from the party tray after he had touched some. She certainly isn't going to eat any of her favorite fudge after he has mauled it. More for him that way. He eats it for breakfast and lunch and for little hourly snacks. He washes it down with pineapple juice.

"You know, I'm thirsty all the time," he says. "That's a sign of diabetes."

"Your one doctor already told you you had diabetes. The new one wanted to get your heart straight first," she tells him. The Florida doctor had warned her about his blood sugar, and at first she had tried to make the right meals for the old man. Both of her grandmothers had diabetes, and she doesn't want to get it herself in her old age. She knows the food choices by heart. He lost eight pounds the first two weeks he lived with them. The new doctor said let him eat what he wants. He doesn't have much time left. That was nine months ago.

"Thirsty all the time," he says. "I wake up in the night thirsty."

"Well, if it worries you, you should talk to the doctor about it," she says.

He grunts and waves his fingertips at her, a dismissive wave, something he picked up from his third wife, the one who got the house and all his stuff. The oh-so-devout one who thanks God for giving her an empty parking place near the front of the store, but who couldn't keep her vow to God to stay married to him. Perhaps wife number three is thanking God for the house this Christmas. There's not a lot of thanking going on at his new house, that's for sure. It's not really his house, it's his son's house. The old man has his own room and his own bathroom, his own phone line, TV, cable, computer and everything. He comes downstairs to eat or to see what's going on, trying to stay out of the way, trying to be helpful. Squeak. That's the stair-chair turning around so he can get into it. It doesn't have to squeak. It squeaks because he has the brake halfway engaged all the time. He's been shown how to use it, but he doesn't. Doesn't remember? Doesn't want to? Doesn't care. Squeak. Then a groan as he sits.

"Does he groan like that all the time?" his doctor asked her on one visit. She nodded. "Then let me give you something to read."

Later she read the brochure on choosing a nursing home, something neither she nor her husband, the old man's son, want to have to do. The old man would surely die in a nursing home. He's living just fine now, if only they could be more patient. Perhaps they could try and entertain him more, engage in more real conversations, perhaps even talk about something other than doctors and medicine.

"How cold did it get last night?" the old man asks.

"I don't know. I didn't look," she says.

"I usually get that on the computer, but it's gone," he

says.

"What's gone?"

"The weather. It used to be right there, and now it's gone."

"Your settings must have gotten changed. You can pick what's on that front page. The home page."

"Well, I didn't change anything," he says. Defensive. Afraid to be wrong.

"I'm not saying you did," she answers, although she knows it has to be something he did, even if he did it inadvertently. Settings don't just change on their own.

"I didn't do anything to it," he says.

"It's easy to fix. I'll do it for you after while," she says. "Don't worry about it."

He wanders around the kitchen, the dining room, looking for something sweet. She could pull out the caramel corn her mother made special for them for Christmas, one big bag for her, one for her husband. The old man has already eaten one of the bags, taking it up to his room. "I get hungry up there at night," he says. Yes, she could pull out that second bag of caramel corn, but she doesn't. She has hidden it behind the empty jars in the pantry, knowing that he will probably find it anyway.

"He can't find a gallon of milk sitting right in front of him in the refrigerator," her husband says. "How can he find something you hide?"

Radar, she thinks to herself, but she just shrugs.

It was Santa radar they used to check at her parents' house, driving three or six or even twenty hours from wherever they were living at the time to spend Christmas with her family. It had taken the newlyweds only one Christmas with his family to decide how they were going to split up the holidays: New Year's with his family, Christmas with hers.

At her husband's, his mother, the first wife, in an attempt to be perfectly fair, would get everyone the same gift. Identical billfolds for the daughters-in-law, but different colors, and sweaters of the same style. The boys would get sweaters and something else, all the same, as if dressing for a family portrait. She'd put each person's gifts, no matter how many, into one box to open. The gifts were barely unwrapped before his parents breathed a sigh of relief, "Well, THAT'S over," and stuffed the already-decorated tree back into its cardboard box.

At her house, presents were piled up under the tree and wrapped to fool and confuse. A shirt wrapped in a box with a brick. A paperback slid down into a fat wrapping paper tube. A pair of socks wrapped separately. There were plates of homemade cookies and candy and nuts and meals fit for royalty.

When their son was born, they continued to drive all night for Christmas, and Santa always seemed to find him at his grandparents' house. They'd listen to the radio reports of Santa being spotted on radar, and while the little boy slept, Santa left his gifts under his grandparents' tree. By Christmas afternoon when the cousins arrived, the family room was a jumble of GI Joes and Transformers and He-men, and all the adults would be recovering from a sleepless night of drinking beers from around the world and applying scores of decals to some-assembly-required toys.

But not this year. This year Santa will have to find their son in Korea doing whatever it is a new soldier does on his first Christmas away from home. And she's not taking the old man on a ten-hour drive to her folks'.

It's Christmas Eve now, and the fudge is gone. She could make another batch, but she doesn't. She's out of the mood. It's Christmas Eve, and it's just the three of them.

She turns on the Christmas tree lights and sinks into the couch in the family room. The blinkers flash green, white, and red against the slick silver paper of the presents piled under the tree. She wants to believe this year the old man might like his presents, but she knows better. "Don't take it personally," her husband tells her. "He never does."

Once the boy's mother tried to surprise the old man with a ukulele, which he said he'd played as a kid. He half unwrapped it and told her to take it back. It is his pattern. It is a wonder anyone still tries to please him. He hates Christmas. As a boy he got a present from the Boy Scouts— an apple and an orange. He slipped one piece of fruit into the stocking of each of his brothers. That was all they got that year. After that he must have quit trying. The third wife was devastated when he gave her money on Christmas morning and told her, "Go buy yourself a little something." She decided he didn't love her, and perhaps he didn't. But that wasn't why he did what he did Christmas morning. He holds a grudge against Christmas because it had the nerve to come along during the depression. And now, decades later, it's like it was yesterday to him.

Perhaps we should get him some fruit, she wants to say to her husband, but she doesn't. Not out loud anyway. Having his father live with them is a strain on him, too. A double burden. He has to watch the man who raised him deteriorate before his eyes, and he has to watch what pater familias is doing to his wife. She hates it when the old man treats her husband like a boy and her like an object.

"He's an old man," they whisper to each other under the covers in the night in their own room, never sure what the old man can hear with his selective hearing. "He can't help it."

Sometimes she thinks he can help it. She thinks he

is in a world he created by driving the women around him crazy and then standing back and asking what happened, like a Labrador cocking his head to examine the remains of a knocked over lamp. Is it his life that's there in pieces on the floor or the lives of those around him?

The phone rings. The line is clear and sharp.

"Merry Christmas, Mom."

"Jason! Where are you?" she says, although she knows where he is, in Yongsan. She only imagines his little on-base apartment with its two-burner kitchen.

"Where do you think, Mom?" he says. She can hear his smile.

"Your dad just ran out for a bit," she says. "He'll be sorry he missed you."

"He's probably shopping for your present," he says.

"Did you get my package?" she asks.

"Yeah, thanks. I particularly love the socks with Christmas fish on them. Like I don't get enough redneck cracks being from Georgia."

She laughs. She's missed that about him. She's missed all of him.

"Did you get Grandpa some, too?"

In the mirror over the mantle she sees her face draw tight into a frown, or is it a scowl? She forces a smile at her reflection.

"Don't try to worm information out of me on Christmas Eve," she says. "You know I'll never tell."

"It's always worth a try," he says. "Hey, did Grandpa tell you he sent me a letter?"

Did he say something and she ignored it? Did he do it on his own, get a stamp and walk to the mailbox?

"He wrote how proud he was about flight school and everything, and he said he'd always wanted to fly helicopters.

He sent me a check, too."

She watches the tree lights blink on, then off.

"Is he there, Mom? Can I talk to him?"

She carries the portable phone upstairs and says goodbye to her son. From the kitchen she can hear the old man laughing, asking questions. Animated. Engaged.

In a box in their bedroom closet there is another letter from the old man, creased from so many foldings and unfoldings, the paper soft with age. It is a letter of congratulations for being the first in the family to graduate from college, for sticking with it when the old man feared the young married couple would have other priorities, for being the son he was so proud of. Is so proud of.

The chair squeaks. The old man groans. The chair whirs. He's bringing down the portable phone.

She has a few more packages to wrap. Homemade gifts to deliver in the neighborhood. A chicken ready for roasting sits in the refrigerator, but it doesn't seem so special anymore. She remembers standing in the old man's backyard where, with a beer in one hand and tongs in the other, he pontificated on the perfectly grilled steak. Her mother-in-law winked and whispered, "Never learn to light the grill." The boy without even a piece of fruit in his own stocking became a man who could feed his family steak and send his middle child to college.

He hands her the phone and lowers himself onto a bar stool at the kitchen counter. She rummages around in the walk-in pantry for the bag of caramel corn.

"I thought it was all gone," he says, fumbling with the twist tie on the bag. He grabs a handful then dumps the rest in the bowl she set out.

"I've been thinking about supper, Dad," she says. "Would you mind if we grilled some steaks instead of the baked chicken?"

"You know to get the ones with the most marbling," he says. He pushes caramel corn into his mouth with the heel of his hand and chews.

"Why don't you help pick them out?"

He looks at the caramel corn and back at her.

"Not right now," she says. "Later, when Bill gets home. The two of you can go. And get some of those big potatoes to bake."

"And some sour cream," he says. "The old kind, not that low-fat stuff."

"Sure, why not?" she says. Why not indeed. It's Christmas after all. And it's the three of them.

CHAPERONE FOR COUSIN KATIE

Calvin and my cousin Katie sat in the front of his navy blue Camaro with the wide white stripes on the hood practically getting impaled on the gear shifter while they made out from their respective bucket seats. I sat in the back. Supposedly I was like a chaperone or something. I was just happy to be included.

Calvin disconnected his lips from my cousin's face long enough to point at the sky that was darker and bluer than his new Levi's.

"There's not enough stars in the world to give you," he said.

"Oh, Calvin," Katie said, with that kind of breathless voice I'd watched her practice in front of her bedroom mirror, scrunching up her lips and flipping her blonde hair just like Marilyn Monroe.

Romantic it wasn't. I know Katie thought he was just to die for, but I wasn't impressed. Calvin was on the dim side compared to her former boyfriends. He had a nice car, and he was working so he had money to spring for popcorn at the drive-in or a root beer float at the Dog 'n Suds, but he lacked depth, and evidently, even a rudimentary knowledge of astronomy. Stars were outside of the world, that's why they called it outer space. My opinion, however, wasn't even a blip on the radar. I was the little cousin with the blue plastic glasses like cats-eyes who knew nothing about boys. I take that back. I knew plenty about boys as brothers. I was ignorant in the ways of boyfriends.

Calvin opened his car door, and the dome light momentarily blinded me. I looked down at the vinyl mat on the floor, and I felt rather than saw him reach around behind his seat to pull the seatback toward him, squishing himself against the steering wheel.

"Take a walk," he said.

"Now?" It was dark, and the weeds along this dirt road were knee high. No telling what was lurking in there.

"How about I just close my eyes?" I said. "I won't even listen."

"For God's sake, Amanda, just get out of the car!" Katie said.

I made it to the front fender, then stopped.

"What's wrong with you?" Calvin said to me. He stuck his head out the window.

"She's scared," Katie said. She may have been whispering, but the night was still as a coiled snake. I could hear her fine.

"Scared of the dark," she added.

I'd have been insulted, if it wasn't true. I rubbed the toe of my tennis shoe in little circles by the tire.

"Turn on the lights," Katie said.

"They'll drain the battery," he said.

"Then we better go," she said. She shifted around in

her seat. I knew what she was doing. She was crossing her arms in that way she did when she put her foot down. End of story.

"Okay, geez," he said.

The lights made long shadows of the tall weeds. There was dust hanging inches above the road, like a car had only moments before passed this way, but I knew there was no one on this road but us. The lights were two strong beams, searching into the future down the narrow road, following the ruts before intersecting somewhere above the grassy runner in the middle where tires almost never rolled. No one really pulled off the road around here. They just drove until they were alone and parked. I knew what parking was. After all, I was in junior high now. Practically grown.

I walked a little ways. On either side of the beams everything was even darker than before. Flying bugs near the edge of the road were flapping white wings. One collided with my forehead, and I turned around. The back of Katie's head was up against the windshield. How did she do that? She could be one of those acrobats on the Ed Sullivan show, wearing those white tights and spinning around. She could be lots of things, but Katie just wanted to be Calvin's girlfriend. She wore his old class ring on a chain around her neck until it started to leave green lines on her skin. Then she wrapped adhesive tape around and around the bottom part, the part you don't really see when it's on your finger. She covered the tape with yarn, and then she wore it on her middle finger. She changed the yarn every day to match her outfits. Today it was pink to go with the sleeveless shell that showed off her figure. Katie said I'd get a figure like hers one day, because we were related. But I wasn't so sure. We were like those two pictures her dad showed us when he took a shot with his Land camera and pulled off the backing. Positive and negative. She was blonde to my brunette. She was softly curved like a road around the lake, where I was more like an intersection in town, all right angles and straight lines. Mother nature was going to have to do quite a bit in the next two years if I was going to look like her.

Her hair, which I had watched her rat and poof and smooth into a little flip right below her ears, caught the green of the dash lights. So did her now bare shoulders that were bobbing up and down in the passenger seat like she was on a runaway carousel horse. I sat down on the dirt facing away from the car until I heard Calvin grind away at his starter and the car engine turn over.

"Let's go, squirt," he said. He opened the car door. The dome light was dimmer, kind of yellowish, then it brightened up. He grinned, but not at me. He looked half asleep.

Katie had her compact out, and her rat-tail comb. She poked the tail into her hairdo at random points, lifting it out where it had been smooshed. She put on fresh lipstick, while I climbed in the back seat. Calvin closed the door and the light went out.

All the lights were on at her house when Calvin pulled into the driveway. Our parents were playing Tripoli, and through the open windows we could hear the ratchety click of plastic poker chips rubbing up against each other. A quick kiss between them, and he backed the car out onto the highway, leaving Katie and me standing in the shadows of the sidewalk.

"One word," she said, pinching my arm at that tender part just inside the elbow, "and I swear you'll be toast."

This time I was insulted. What did she take me for? I was no snitch. I snatched my arm back and stormed up the steps. She followed me into the kitchen and got two Cokes out of the fridge.

"Open these, while I get some chips," she said.

Her dad came in, carrying a full ashtray and an empty glass.

"Have a nice time did you, girls?" he said.

"Yes, Daddy," Katie said. She smiled past him with a metal tray of potato chips and French onion dip. We could never take food to our rooms in my house. Katie did it all the time. She put the tray on her dressing table and locked the door. She put a finger perpendicular to her lips. Her nails were short and gnawed, something her pearl pink polish couldn't camouflage.

I took a drink of my Coke and my lips made that farting noise against the lip of the bottle by accident.

Katie was bending over in her closet looking for something. She glared at me from between her knees. She could definitely be on the Ed Sullivan show.

"Did you ever think of being an acrobat?" I asked her.

"What, like in the circus?" she said. "What do you take me for?"

I plowed a chip across the surface of the dip. Katie emerged from the closet with a boxy pink overnight case. I had one just like it, only mine was blue. Christmas presents from our grandmother. Inside they had little elastic pockets and a mirror set at a jaunty angle.

"Are you going home with me?" I said. I loved having sleepovers with Katie, but mostly I stayed at her house. She had a big collection of *Teen Magazine*, which was usually strewn about her room, and there were a few worn copies of *True Confessions* hidden inside her math and biology workbooks from last year.

Katie put the suitcase on the bed. The latches snapped

back against the lid. The suitcase was packed. On top was a thin white nightgown with lace at the neck. She'd never worn something like that at my house before. I reached out to touch it, and she smacked my hand.

"Dip!" she said.

I looked at my fingers. Sure enough, there was some French onion dip. I sucked it off.

"Where did you . . ." I started to say, but she interrupted.

"It was a present from Calvin," she said. "For our wedding night."

"Wed . . ." I managed to get out before she clamped a sweaty palm against my mouth.

"Shh," she said. "Tonight. He said we can get a justice of the peace in Kentucky for $5. He's coming back to get me at 10." The hands on her alarm clock said 9:30.

"Do your parents know?" I said, then rolled my eyes at the stupidity of my own question. Katie glared again. For someone who was getting married tonight, she wasn't cutting me much slack. Her parents didn't like Calvin, which is why the unhappy couple got me as a ride-along tonight.

My mom said Katie was boy crazy. My uncle said when Katie was little they were at church and an old man asked her if she had a boyfriend. Katie just sat there doodling on her program for a second, then she said, "Yes, sir, one." She doodled for a few more seconds then looked up at the man and said, "Tell you what. I'm gonna marry him." My uncle laughed when he told that story, and even though at the time of the incident I was still in diapers, and technically couldn't have known Katie's intentions, I'm sure she was dead serious.

Katie was always cool, something that was getting to be more important to me. Katie had answers to questions I hadn't even thought up yet. Without her expertise I would never have made the most of my blue eyes behind my thick glasses.

"They're your best feature," she told me, "and they're hidden."

It was Katie who taught me to roll my hair and to tape my bangs with cellophane so they wouldn't get messed up in the night. I owed her. Now she was trying to collect big time.

"I'm going to say I'm going out to check on the pony," Katie said. "Get it?"

"Not really," I said.

"Pony. You know, Pony car," she said.

When I just stared at her, she looked at the ceiling.

"P - o - n - y car. The Camaro!"

I'd forgotten that Calvin had explained all that to me, about the cars that were made like the Mustang.

"Why don't you just get a Mustang then?" I asked.

"Because I'm a Chevrolet man," he said.

"Okay," I told Katie. "You go to check on the pony."

"And they'll think I'm going to the barn," she said. "I'll really be meeting Calvin."

I nodded. My mouth was full of chips.

"You," she said, "will stay here and drop me my suitcase out the window."

"Then what?"

"Then what? I meet Calvin at the highway, and we get married. He's got a motel room and everything."

"I mean then what, what? Where do you live? Will he drive you to school? What about college?"

Katie pulled at a sticky string of adhesive tape on the edge of Calvin's ring. The yarn was a little ragged now.

"Once we're married they can't tell me what to do,"

she said. "College is their thing, not mine, anyway."

"What's wrong with college?" I had my hopes set on college.

"I'm not going to end up an old maid schoolteacher," she said. "Like you're gonna. No one's letting you teach science, anyway. Have you ever seen a girl science teacher? Answer me that."

I didn't want to teach science, I wanted to do science, but Katie didn't even give me a chance to answer. She just plowed on ahead as if it were a rhetorical question.

"I want more out of life than that," she said.

Katie had plans all right. In home economics class she had made a poster board collage of her dream house. It was all modern and sleek, nothing like the early American furniture at my aunt's house. Sort of like the Jetson's only in color. She must have some kind of a plan.

"What am I supposed to tell your parents when you don't come back from the barn?" I said.

"Nothing." She checked her lipstick in the mirror and rubbed a bit from a tooth.

"So when everyone goes crazy looking for you, I just sit here?"

"Will you stop with the questions, already? Geez, Louise, don't you ever shut up? You're acting so ... immature!"

I scrunched my eyes closed tight so I wouldn't cry. It's not a crime to be curious, is it? When I opened my eyes, she was gone.

I heard a pause in the chatter in the dining room, then the screen door shut. I wiped my nose on my sleeve and leaned out the window, dangling Katie's purse from one hand and her overnight bag from the other. Her own face was scrunched up when she reached for the bags. Perhaps it was the light from the room.

"See ya, squirt," she said, and she disappeared down the drive.

I curled myself around a ruffled pillow on Katie's bed. Already the room felt empty, abandoned. Would she come back for her stuff? What would I tell her parents? Tears leaked out and soaked into the pillowcase. Inside my closed eyelids Katie danced across a wooden stage in a snow white leotard with silver spangled stars, her body twisting and tumbling in a choreographed routine that had the crowd on its feet. She got a running start and did three backwards flips in a row, so fast the spotlight couldn't follow. When the light found her, Katie was standing just offstage in her new white nightgown with the lace at the neck, the silver spangled stars just so much litter at her feet.

LITTLE MISTER

My momma don't want nothing to go to waste or no one to go around without a goodly amount of loving. That's why we wasn't surprised when she bring home that little wiener dog that started all the trouble. I swear, your honor, on a whole stack of Bibles like that black one you got up there, it was that what started it all off.

Don't think I'm fixing to blame my momma. No, sir. It ain't my momma's fault anymore than it's her fault Cliff Claymore don't know that thin line between drunk and sober excepting in his rear view mirror. No, sir, I ain't blaming nobody, I'm just telling you the whole story, the truth and nothing but the truth like that woman there had me swear.

It started on a Tuesday. I know that for a fact because my momma been cleaning the Anderson's house on a Tuesday ever since I remember. And ever Tuesday she bring home something them Andersons didn't want no more. Like maybe flowers that still had a few more days on them. Once it was a perfectly good sweeper what just needed a belt and some oil. There's plenty of Tuesdays all stacked up in my memory, Judge, and there was a lot of shit stacked up at our house that started out in their big house. Beg pardon, sir, that "shit" just came out on accident. That gal from the public defender done warned me about that. As I was saying, my momma brung home that dog she say they don't want no more cause it done bark all the time and pee on their carpet.

"That's nice, Momma," I says, real polite-like. She raised me to be polite. "But what's gonna stop that dog from barking and peeing on our floor?"

"I'll be training him," she says, and then she says to the dog, "Ain't that right, Little Mister?" You could tell that dog just love my momma. He look up at her and let out one yip, smiled a big old wiener dog smile and wagged his curly-q tail. Next he hiked up one back paw and peed on my shoe. That's the way it was gonna be, your honor. That dog done figured out day one which side his bread was buttered on. He got nothing but smiles for my momma. I just told you what he got for me.

You already know about my troubles, cause the police told me you got my whole file, your honor, and I do apologize. I had me a mean temper back when I drank, but I ain't had a drop in four years, god's honest truth. It wasn't my nature to walk away from nothin', and I got a scar to this day right here on my forehead from that bouncer's ring down at the Voodoo Lounge. Don't get me wrong, I ain't no saint. But I ain't drinking none, either. I been going to the meetings. I ain't hit no one what didn't deserve it in a long time. Cliff Claymore will vouch for that, judge.

So here it was a Friday, what you called "the day in question." I was just coming out the Kwik-Pick with a pack of smokes. I always get them there because they's a nickel cheaper. And there was Cliff Claymore setting in his Buick

Riviera in the parking lot. He had his nose stuck in the ashtray running change around in there with his pointing finger. He was moving his lips, so I knows he was counting. I been there, done that, your honor. Cliff, he work real hard laying asphalt, making them driveways for all the Wendy's and such, but his paycheck don't last from one Friday to the next. That cheap so-and-so Franklin what he works for don't hand out the checks until quitting time on Friday. So Cliff was fishing for change, and I wasn't doing nothing that couldn't be interrupted. I opened the passenger door and hopped in.

"Smoke?" I offered him a cancer stick.

"Hell, yes, you see me digging for nickels?" he says.

"Nickels don't buy squat," I told him. "What we need is some dollars."

"I heard that," Cliff says, leaning back in his seat. He blowed the smoke out like he was smoking a cigar. "I don't know what's worse. Gas at three bucks a gallon or smokes at five bucks a pack."

"I heard that." We smoked a while, and then I remembered I had something to do for my momma.

"Cliff, I gotta get myself over at the vet's office and pick up something."

Cliff, he didn't need asking about a ride, he just started up the old Buick and backed her onto the street. There weren't but one vet in town, Doc Brown.

We get there, I tell Cliff I won't be a minute, and he says okay by him, but do I have an extra five on me for a pint? I had a twenty of my momma's in my pocket earlier. Before I got the smokes.

"Maybe so," I says. "Depends on how much Doc gonna charge me."

They got a little bell rings when you open the door

at the vets, but I swear I never understood why. Ever time that bell rings there's a bunch of dogs in the back just go to howling. The girl at the desk was setting bottles of shampoo in little rows, like they was bowling pins just waiting to get mowed down.

"Steeerike," I says. I did my arm like this, your honor, like I just laid a perfect hook ball on the lane, and I balanced there on one foot just smiling when that girl turn around and look at me with her head cocked to the side like one a them TV commercial dogs. Like she was saying, "What the hell?" Sorry, Judge, but that's just how she look.

"You got something held for my momma," I says real quick, but polite. "Mrs. Bessie Fisher. That's my momma."

"What is it?" she asks.

"I don't rightly know," I says. "She just said 'pick it up.'"

The girl just tilted her head again and clicked her pen against her teeth. "Wait here," she says.

She opened a door to the back and them dogs started howling again. I didn't hear no bell this time, but maybe it was one of them silent bells just for dogs.

Right by the desk there was a cork board with pictures of dogs on it, and I was wondering if just anyone could bring a picture of their dog and tack up there. I thought Momma would be proud to have a picture of Little Mister there. Maybe I'd surprise her and take one in there myself for her birthday or something. Then I got to noticing the writing under some of them pictures. "Stud service." "AKC champion." When I read what they was charging for them dogs for just a few minutes of their time—some of them dogs was getting $500 a shot—it was like a light bulb going off. Momma's dog had to have papers. Them Andersons wouldn't a had no mutt. I find the papers, I'd be in business. Wouldn't

Momma be surprised when she seen all that money?

That girl come out with a see-through pouch with something red and white inside. "Here's the sweater your mother ordered, Mr. Fisher."

A sweater for a dog? Now I seen everything.

"That will be $16.45 with tax."

I felt my pocket for what was left of the twenty, knowing full well that after the smokes I only had a ten and a five.

"Are you sure she didn't already pay for it? Since she ordered it special?"

"I tell you what, I'll check with doctor later. If she still owes, I'll send a bill." The girl sure was pretty, even if she did keep hitting her front teeth with that pen. I wondered if she ever got the wrong end up and inked her teeth. It didn't look like it.

"That'd be just fine, Miss," I says. "By the way, what's the other name for a wiener dog?"

"You mean the dachshund?"

"That's it. Can you write that down on a piece a paper there?" She wrote it out nice and plain on a paper with "Flea Be Gone" printed on the top. Then I borrowed her pen and wrote Momma's phone number real big on the bottom and put STUD FEE $300. I didn't want to be greedy. She just watched me write it all out and put it on the board. When I left she set there at the desk with her head cocked just tapping them teeth.

It didn't take long for Cliff Claymore to catch my drift about the stud service. We was sitting in the Buick in my momma's driveway. I could hear that wiener dog just barking inside.

"Hell, you gonna be a rich man," Cliff says. "Don't be forgetting your friends when you get flush, man."

"I ain't gonna get that rich. Not Trump rich. I aim to be the same as I am now. Just have me all the smokes I want and a pizza now and then what don't come out of a freezer."

That dog was up in the picture window standing on the back of the couch pawing the glass, barking. I wondered how he'd look in that sweater. Probably like a Christmas candy cane.

"I gotta get in there and find those papers," I tells Cliff. Then I remembers the change in my pocket. I pull out a ten. "Here, Cliff. Get yourself something and come on back. You can help me look."

First thing that dog do is try and squeeze through that screen door and get out front. I push him back in the house with my foot, gentle-like, then he grab my shin with them sharp black claws and pee on my sock. This keep up I'm gonna have to wear my old Army boots.

Momma keeps her important papers in a big wood box on the kitchen counter that says: "The Andersons, Bob and Peggy," on the side in burned-in letters. Them dog papers wasn't in there. They wasn't in her bedroom, either, or under the couch cushions. I was on my knees looking under the couch when they called. They wanted to know all about the wiener dog and his papers and stuff. I tells them . . . them people sitting right over there, your honor. That's them. The plaintiffs. I tells them all about the dog, and they's asking me could I fetch him over to meet their dog. And I tells them yes, but I'm gonna need the money up front. I wanted them to know I wasn't borned yesterday. They say it gonna depend on if the dogs like each other and about his pedigree. Now I didn't know what part was his pedigree, but whatever it was, I was sure it was just in dandy shape. Like I says before, the Anderson's don't buy no junk.

It was Cliff's idea to put the candy cane outfit on him. Cliff has him some good ideas when he's drinking. I used to myself, back in the day. I know what you're thinking, Judge, but I didn't touch a drop. Cliff done finished off the bottle before he got back to my momma's house, anyway. Said he didn't want to tempt me none, being as I was quit and all. I sweared to tell the truth, and I am.

That wiener dog didn't much like that outfit. Cliff and I both had to hold him down to get it snapped. I think that dog knowed it was Cliff's idea, cause soon as we was done he bit Cliff on the ankle and peed on his shoe. He might a changed his opinion on Cliff when we got in the car. That dog did like riding in a car. He hopped up and down and stuck his head out the window and barked. His ears was flapping against his head so hard I thought he might knock his own brains out. I had to hold on his back legs to keep him from flying out.

We got there, and there was a chain link fence like they said. We parked in the gravel and first thing their girl wiener dog comes running down the sidewalk barking her fool head off. Momma's Little Mister was jumping and barking, too.

"So far, so good," I says to Cliff. He squeezed his eyes tight together and nodded. Cliff be feeling good. Bourbon do that.

"Why don't you just hang out here, Cliff, and I'll be right back," I tells him. Truth be told, I think he was relieved. He got blood on his sock from earlier.

I had a hard time holding onto Little Mister cause he was fixing to get down and see that girl dog, but I wasn't about to let him do his business there without cash on the barrelhead, if you know what I mean, Judge. So I kept hold of him best I could, him biting my fingers and scratching my belly while that girl dog nipped at my knees, trying to get at him.

That's when the screen door slammed back against the house and them people come running out.

"Keep him away from our Petunia," they hollered. I was already holding him so tight his eyeballs was bugging out.

"Howdy," I says. "This here's Little Mister."

They scooped up their dog like they was a giant Dust Buster and motioned for me to come on the porch. We sat there across from each other a holding dogs for dear life.

"Well, she certainly seems to be interested," she says.

"She'd be interested in a German Shepherd at this point," he says. "We should have picked out a stud BEFORE she went into heat."

"Well, guess who was just too busy watching football to do THAT?" she ask.

I figured this was one a them ongoing things, your honor, so I ask if we can just settle up before Little Mister do the deed. You'd a thought I had a gun to their heads. They start in about that pedigree again and ask for a bunch of papers, and when I tell them he my momma's dog and I couldn't find no papers, they get downright nasty. They trashed Little Mister. Call him a mutt. Say his eyes is too close to his nose and his legs is too long.

You know there ain't no love lost between me and that dog, Judge, but it's one thing to have trouble in the family, and it's something else for strangers to sound off like that. I squeezed Little Mister even tighter and stomped down them steps toward the Buick. That she-devil Petunia chased us all the way.

"We're outta here," I says to Cliff, and I slam the gate shut behind me. Cliff put her in gear to back out when

Petunia push open the gate and run up to the car.

"Don't squash her," I yells at Cliff. He slams on the brakes. Little Mister jumps out the window right that second, and I grab for him and catch the sweater. He hangs there in midair for a second, and then he spins around like that girl in *The Exorcist* and hops right out a that candy cane thing. Before I can open the door him and Petunia is going at it longside the road.

Petunia's daddy, well he comes flying off the porch swinging a metal baseball bat at Little Mister. He ain't got good aim so he hits the gravel by his girl dog instead. She yelps and them stuck-together dogs scoot underneath the Buick. Just for safety, I figure. They don't seem to care none about privacy. Then the wife, she starts smacking her husband in the chest with her fists, cause that's only how far up she can reach. And he turns around to swing at her, but breaks his swing at the last minute and hits the car instead. I could a told him that wasn't a smart thing to do when Cliff Claymore's been drinking, but nobody asked me, and then the man scoots underneath the car in the gravel trying to poke at them dogs with the bat. Cliff, he stretches his long arms up in the air like he's gonna make a jump shot, and then he tosses me the car keys.

"Open the trunk," he says, and I barely gets it open when he drags the man out from under the car by his ankles. Cliff steps on the husband's bat-hand so he lets go, and then grabs him by the scruff of the neck and shoves him in the trunk. I ain't never seen so much banging in my life. The man's banging inside the trunk, them dogs is banging underneath the car, and she's banging on the trunk lid.

"Get out here if you know what's good for you, you good for nothing so-and-so," she be yelling at him like he could unlock it from inside. I'd a stayed in there, too, I was him. After a while them dogs was done, and Little Mister just crawls over and falls dead asleep on my shoe. Cliff Claymore let the husband out. The woman, she reach under the car and put Petunia in a carry pouch she make with the bottom of her shirt. I was just asking for what was due me when the woman go inside and call the po-lice.

No, your honor, I don't think they seen any humor in that. That's why they file them charges and done get me hauled in here like a criminal when it be me and Little Mister been wronged. They owes us $300. I got them papers now. And Little Mister, he did the deed. They got the pups to prove it.

ROOMMATES

OB arrived mid-semester carrying a ragged black guitar case with a BLAME GE sticker on the side, an overstuffed backpack, and a mesh onion bag full of hotel soaps. I got back from lunch and there he was, sitting on the empty bed in my room.

He waved a yellow room assignment sheet, and I stuck out my hand to shake.

"I'm Brad," I told him.

It took him few seconds to transfer the paper to his other hand, an awkward pause I'd soon come to recognize.

"OB." He swallowed the letters as he spoke. He folded the yellow paper into matchbook size and dropped it on the bare bed with at least a dozen others of similar configuration. He began to sort them into piles.

"Obi? Like in Obi-Won Kenobi?" I asked.

He didn't look up. "Yeah, right. Or Opie from *Andy Griffith*. Whatever."

"OB as in what, then? Obstetrician?"

He dipped his head and gave it a quick shake to the side to get his blonde hair out of his eyes. He stared at my face.

"Oliver Baxter. Tell me you wouldn't be OB?" He went back to sorting.

"Yeah, man. I'd be OB."

He unzipped the backpack and upended it on the bed. I watched him unpack. He scooped up a slew of folded papers and dumped them in his middle desk drawer. His clothes were all black, even his underwear, and he put each piece away one at a time, as if he had to think about it. He had three books with homemade brown paper covers that he stashed on the shelf of his desk and a dozen or so spiral notebooks with inked warnings on the outside, like "Read This and Die" and "Keep Out, This Means You."

"Journals?" I asked him.

"What?" he said.

"The notebooks," I nodded toward his desk. "You keep a journal? I tried it, but I couldn't stay awake."

"Stories," he said.

"You're a writer? Cool," I said. "So's my girlfriend."

"You?" he said.

"History and phys ed. Secondary ed."

OB opened his guitar case. His guitar looked like a yellow mummy, tightly wrapped in cloth that turned out to be his sheets. He examined the instrument for damage, pinged each string, then returned it to the case. He was making his bed, checking each corner twice, when a football came flying through the open door, bounced, and rolled end-to-end toward his feet. My friends Zebo and Henry followed it in and headed for their usual spot on the spare bed when they ran smack into OB. OB turned on a dime, his hands up in a boxer's pose.

"Whoa," Zebo said. "New occupant." He stuck out his hand.

"Zebo," he said to OB. "I'm down the hall. This ugly one here," he pointed at Henry, "is my roommate Henry. Like Indiana Jones only not as lucky."

Henry stuck out his hand, too.

"Meet my new roommate, OB," I said.

OB lowered one arm, then the other, but his feet were still planted. He looked from Zebo to Henry and back to Zebo, and finally extended a hand to Zebo, pumping two firm shakes. He repeated the process with Henry.

"We're late for a scrimmage," Zebo said. "Want to join us?"

OB looked to me, not for approval or an invitation, but as if he expected me to handle his regrets. He barely shook his head; it was more of a wobble.

"Let the guy get settled in before you start breaking bones," I said. I picked up the ball and tossed it from hand to hand.

OB turned back to his sheets, pulling them so tight you could see the design in the mattress pad. As I went out the door, I saw OB put the bag of soaps into his pillowcase.

It didn't take long for word to spread that mine wasn't the party room anymore. OB wasn't just quiet, it was like he wasn't even there except for that constant low-volume buzz from his headphones. He had jack adapters to switch from his guitar to his iPod without uncovering his ears. He was always plugged in to something.

"You think he takes them off to shower?" Zebo said. We were standing in line for lunch.

I had to think about it for a minute.

"I don't think I've ever seen him in the shower," I said. When I said it there was a twinge, just a little one, in the pit of my stomach, like I had betrayed some confidence.

"Christ, doesn't he stink?" Zebo said.

I shrugged. Actually, our room smelled better than my room ever had. Since it wasn't the party room anymore, it smelled less like old pizza and beer and more like, I don't know, clean, like a bedroom, like Candice's dorm room. I was spending a lot more time in her room since OB arrived, but that didn't stop her from dropping in on OB and me as if our room was just an annex of her own.

"Do you think it smells in here?" I asked her that afternoon when she stopped in after class.

Candice sniffed the air like a bird dog.

"Your Converses," she said, pointing at the high tops I had taken off and thrown in the corner.

"Nothing else?"

Candice sniffed again, then buried her face in my neck. "Just your pheromones," she said.

I checked my watch to see how much time we had before OB came back from class. Not long enough. I swung my feet off the bed and got us some bottled water from the little fridge that used to be full of beer. OB opened the door just when I cracked the plastic seal around the lid.

He nodded at me, smiled at Candice, and dropped a Fed-X box and his book bag on the bed. He pulled out a handful of folded notes from the pockets of his jeans and arranged them end to end on the edge of his desk like the cars of a model train.

"Goodies from home?" I asked.

"Computer," OB said. He pulled the tab on the package and slid a Macbook out onto his bed. As he sorted through the packaging, he paused, as if bewildered by the cords and accessories, but then plugged in each piece without reading the directions. He did that a lot, just froze. Not like a robot, more like an old man lost in space, or time. OB punched a few keys and let it run. He nodded to us again and left.

"He's brilliant, you know," Candice said. They were in a writing class together. "He read a story today that knocked my socks off." She wiggled her bare toes in her flip flops, as if to prove her point.

"I didn't think he had it in him," I said.

"He's brilliant," Candice repeated.

"He's strange," I said. In our two years together, she'd never called me brilliant.

"We all are," she said. I didn't know if she meant all writers, or all humans.

"Speak for yourself," I said, flashing her a big smile.

"I was," she said, narrowing her eyes just a bit. I guess she meant writers after all.

Regardless of his prowess with the pen, OB wasn't much with the spoken word. After three weeks I knew less about him than I did the dorm's receptionist. It was as if he had just conjured himself out of thin air. Except for that initial backpack, the rest of his stuff came by delivery service, a piece at a time, all new.

"So what gives with the goth?" Zebo said. We were stretching against the wall, waiting for our racquetball court to open up.

"Just because he wears black doesn't mean he's a goth," I said. "You see any nail polish or lipstick?"

"He's definitely Abby Normal. I couldn't live with him."

The court smelled like sweat and rubber, and my shoes squeaked against the maple boards. Zebo did a victory dance when I slid across the floor on my belly only to miss a low shot on the front wall. I slammed into the wall and heard the crunch as my finger jammed the drywall. He strummed his racquet like a guitar, and I couldn't help but compare his sausage-like fingers to the thin bones of OB's hands caressing his Fender. I shook my head, as if, like an upside down etch-a-sketch, I could get a clean slate. I pulled on my jammed finger as Zebo served again.

Candice was in the room when I got back, hunched over OB's computer at his desk. Candice worked the mouse, and OB watched her face as she read. I knew that look. It was the same one I wore when I watched Candice do anything, waiting for her eyes to light up or her brow to furrow, or the pale skin around her freckles to flush. They were sharing his chair, one skinny cheek from each of them meeting in the middle, with not that much overhang. I walked over and kissed her on the back of the neck, and she held up one finger, like "wait," and she kept reading. I sat on my bed and made a lot of noise opening my mail then laughed to myself a couple of times. They didn't move. Finally I saw Candice get to the end. She dropped her hands to her lap and just sat there. When she turned sideways to look at OB, I could see tears.

"I can't tell you how moved I was," Candice said.

"Did the ending work? Was it too quick?" OB said. His headphones were around his neck.

"It was perfect," she said, wiping her face with the hem of her shirt. I got a peek at the bottom of her bra.

"Brilliant," she said.

So, was that her word now? Brilliant?

Candice got up, stretched, and rubbed her rear end.

"My butt went to sleep," she said to me. "Kiss it and make it better?"

Another day I'd have taken that as an invitation. Today it felt more like "kiss my ass."

"Not without a tetanus shot," I said.

Candice parted her lips and frowned at me.

"And your problem is . . ." she said.

"No problems here," I said.

She gave me that stare again, like I was the one who had done something wrong, and she grabbed her backpack off my bed and slung it over one shoulder.

"Later," she said. She waved her hand in front of OB, who was now propped against his headboard, typing away, headphones securely in place.

"See you in class," she said. He smiled. She smiled. She left.

After dinner OB stretched out on his bed and read Kafka, and I waited around for Candice to study with me like she did most nights. At nine, I figured she wasn't going to show. I carried my history textbook down the hall to Zebo and Henry's. They had a twelve-pack and were watching *The Civil War* by Ken Burns on DVD.

"Help yourself," Zebo pointed to the beer carton on the floor. It was warm, but Zebo swore the Europeans liked lukewarm beer. For some reason I doubt that included Old Milwaukee. I passed.

"Think we have time to watch all nine episodes before the test tomorrow?" Henry said. He looked at the DVD slipcase. "We're on number three."

I shook my head. "You don't think it's going to be that bad, do you?" I said. "I mean, it's not like it's the mid-term."

"My sister took it last year, and she said the tests get worse after the mid-term," Zebo said. "Dates, times, names, battlefields. You name it. And he expects a brilliant essay on top of it all."

My stomach felt a little queasy. Brilliant. It reminded

me of the spat with Candice. Maybe the beer wasn't a bad idea after all. I opened a warm can and opened my throat. The faster it went down the less I'd taste.

"Where's Candice?" Henry said.

I shrugged.

Four beers and three hours later I lurched toward bed. OB sat cross-legged on his bedspread, the glow from his computer screen lighting him up like a spook house ghoul.

"Don't you ever turn that damn thing off?" I said. I switched on my desk light. "How am I supposed to sleep?"

"Sorry," OB said. He closed the laptop and put on his sandals. He adjusted the straps individually. I rolled onto my back and rubbed my feet together, trying to get my high-tops off without untying them. I rubbed so hard I thought I smelled burning rubber. I was about to get up for scissors to cut the laces when OB reached for one foot and pinned it to the bed.

"You're drunk," he said, untying my laces.

"No shit, Sherlock," I said. "What was your first clue?"

I sat up on my elbows and took off my shoes. I threw one, then the other, against the far wall. OB put his laptop in his book bag and left. When I woke up, Zebo had his hands on my shoulders, bouncing me on my own bed.

"It's 20 'til," he said. "You planning on taking the test?"

My tongue was stuck to my soft palate, which is all that kept me from cursing. Good thing I slept in my clothes. I knocked two Tic Tacs out of the box for breakfast. The test was a mother. I told myself it would have been the same with or without the beer, but I really couldn't be sure. After, I saw OB coming up the steps.

"About last night," I said.

He didn't say anything.

"You know," I said.

He nodded and hunched his shoulders to reposition his backpack.

I gave him what I hoped was a sheepish smile. I almost heard the "baa" myself. He nodded again and walked on. What was I supposed to get from that? Probably that all was straight. No problem.

Zebo had a different theory. He stopped in our room after dinner.

"He's a psycho, man. I mean, look." Zebo pointed at OB's desk with everything lined up according to size. He yanked open the middle drawer. "And all these little papers folded like notes from junior high. What's with that?"

He started unfolding one, and I stepped in.

"Give him a break," I said. "I wouldn't go through your personal stuff."

"I don't HAVE any personal stuff," Zebo said. "What part of communal living don't you understand?"

I grabbed the paper, and a section ripped off. Zebo raised his hands and backed off. I refolded it as best I could.

He stretched out on OB's bed, and the next thing I knew he pulled the bag of hotel soap from the pillowcase. He dangled it by the twist tie closure.

Inside there dozens of individually wrapped soaps: square cardboard boxes from the fancier hotels, the run-of-the-mill rectangular bars in yellowed paper, translucent pastel egg-shaped soaps, and round ones wrapped in oatmeal-patterned tissue. Zebo pushed the soaps around inside the bag to read the labels. Someone had scrawled dates and places on the wrappers. Las Vegas. Cleveland. Chicago. Pittsburgh.

"For someone who doesn't shower, he's got a load of soap," Zebo said. "It looks like he cataloged them."

"Put it back," I said.

"What are you defending him for?" Zebo said.

"We live together," I said.

"He came from somewhere, he can go somewhere else," Zebo said. "Where was he before this, anyway?"

I shrugged.

"He could have been anywhere. In a nut house. In prison," Zebo said. "His picture could be up in the post office right now."

"For what? Stealing hotel soaps?" I said.

Zebo laughed and stuffed the soap back inside OB's pillowcase, just as Candice walked in.

"Where were you last night?" Zebo said to her. "He came slumming without you."

Candice tossed her hair. "Library," she said. Like that was a good enough explanation. "Have you seen OB?"

"Not since my 11 o'clock," I said. "Why?"

"I promised to bring him something to read," she said. She waved a stapled paper.

"I can give it to him," I said.

"I need to give him the background first," she said. She stuffed it into her backpack. She didn't sit down.

Zebo gave me a look and shuffled out.

"I brought some extra rolls from dinner for our snack for later," I said. I pointed at a plate covered with a brown paper napkin. "I've got some cheese in the fridge."

"I can't stay," she said. "That paper on Bierce is due Monday, and I need something a little extra to pull off what I want to do. A couple of books in Spanish I ordered on loan are in at the library."

"I thought he was an American," I said.

"He disappeared in Mexico, and his body was never found."

"What are you doing, trying to solve the mystery?"

"I'm more interested in his motive for going," she said. She put her hand on the doorknob.

"Maybe later," I said. I gave her a peck on the cheek.

I sprawled out on my bed with *Crime and Punishment*. It was one of those books I just couldn't get into. I didn't read it in high school; I faked my way through the exam with the cliff notes. Now here it was on my syllabus for sociology. I couldn't even keep the characters straight. I wondered if Dostoevsky's life was like that. I'd read that just like his main character, Dostoevsky was hurting for money. Candice said most writers, especially in the beginning, write about things that happened to them, but they have to change it a bit so they don't get sued. She said writers write about what they know. What Dostoevsky knew, though, was boring. If he was supposed to be such a brilliant writer, why couldn't I read more than a page before nodding off? I wondered where my brilliant roommate was. And what his writing was like, besides just being so damned brilliant.

Zebo had a point. I didn't know much about OB. When he got back tonight, I was going to get a few answers.

I must have dozed off, because I woke up with one of those snorts that make you think you were disturbed by your own snoring. OB was at his desk with his laptop and headphones. I tried to read over his shoulder. He slammed the cover down on the laptop and spun in his seat.

"Oh," he said, his eyes focusing on mine. "It's you."

"What you working on?" I said.

"A story," he said.

"What's it about?"

"Hemingway once said that the better the writer the less they'll talk about their own writing," he said. He smiled.

"So you're fucking Hemingway?" I said.

"No," he said. He looked down at his hands and his bangs made a screen over his face. He flipped them to the side and stared at me.

"If I talk about what I'm writing, I can't finish it. It's like," he sighed. "It's like if I say it, I can't write it." He looked up at me and for a second I saw a kid I'd coached in Little League, a skinny white-haired boy with skin so pale his veins showed through, standing there with his batting helmet falling over one ear. The kid with "easy target" embroidered on his sleeve in invisible thread.

My mouth got a little dry. I was being too hard on him. Candice and I had been together a long time. He wasn't trying to weasel in.

"I must have gotten up on the wrong side of the bed," I said. "I didn't mean . . ." Here for the second time today I was apologizing to him. I opened the door to the fridge.

"Cheese?" I pulled out a round of red wax.

He shook his head. I cut myself a chunk and sat back on his bed.

"Got anything that's finished I can read? Candice says you're brilliant." I chugged a bottled water. His face was red and distorted through the plastic.

"That was nice of her," he said. "She's the one with the real talent."

He flipped his bangs to the side again.

"I could print you out something later," he said, "if you're really interested."

He looked at his watch, then stuffed his computer in his backpack. "Seminar," he said, closing the door behind him.

I spent the evening with the guys at the Blue Line Tap, a bar some former student from Chicago opened just off campus. He was known to be a little blind when it came to scrutinizing IDs, as long as you didn't cause any trouble and paid for your drinks in cash. We played pool until we couldn't tell the cue ball from the two ball and were shadowboxing along the sidewalk on the way back when I stopped in my tracks in front of the library. There, lit up like the celebrities on *Hollywood Squares*, Candice and OB sat side by side at a study table, their heads so close together their hair could have intertwined with static electricity.

"Hey, isn't that Candice and the Goth?" Zebo said.

Henry punched him.

"Ow," Zebo said, punching him back.

The two guys rolled in the grass for a minute or so, while I watched OB whisper and Candice laugh and throw her head back like she does to expose her throat. She looked as pale as him in the fluorescent lights. I heard a click, click, and the sprinkler heads poked up out of the library lawn, throwing water high toward the windows and soaking Zebo and Henry. Candice got up and stood by the window, and OB followed. He put his hand on her shoulder. I had seen enough.

"Let's get out of here," I said, breaking into a jog. I saw Candice slipping over the border into Mexico with OB at her side. Holed up in some adobe hut writing their stories together. I nearly ran into a parked car, and Zebo grabbed me.

"Straight ahead," he said, putting his arm around my shoulder. "Follow the yellow brick road."

"It's a sidewalk," Henry said. He took my other side, and the three of us made it back to the dorm with the lurching gait of drunken athletes. We threw ourselves on the floor of my room. They passed my bath towel between them.

"Want us to break his legs?" Henry said.

"Maybe just one," I said.

"Stuff him in the trunk of a car," Zebo said. "If we had a car."

"We could stuff him in the closet," I said.

"He might like that," Henry said. "Don't Goths like to sleep in coffins?"

"I told you he's not a Goth," I said.

"Then what is he?" Henry said. He picked up the emergency flashlight my mom made me bring to school and spun the handle to charge it. It sounded like a toy car revving on the rug. He stuck it under his chin.

"I am vampire," he said like a cartoon ghoul. "I vant to drink your blood."

"And where did he come from?" Zebo said. He crawled over to OB's desk and jerked the drawer open. The whole thing fell out on the floor, the notebooks, and the dozens of folded notes. Zebo threw a handful of notes to Henry.

"Open 'em up. See what he's hiding."

Henry unfolded the first note. It was the syllabus for an art history class. The second one was a flyer for an open mic night at a campus bookstore.

"This is just crap," he said. "Regular stuff."

"Keep going," Zebo said. He was going through the books now. Holding them by their spines and fanning them, looking for anything loose inside that might fall out. A bookmark fluttered to the floor.

Zebo nearly hit me in the head with a notebook he sailed across the room.

"Brad. Check out the notebooks."

The first one was mostly drawings, like comics, snatches of dialogue and lots of swords and fire, with characters taken from video games. OB had marked the notebooks with Roman numerals. Number II was more of the same.

"He was obsessed with *Final Fantasy*," I said.

"Who wasn't?" Henry said. He unfolded another note.

One notebook was filled with yellow and black circles with smiley or frowny faces filled in. Each page had one row of faces in various combinations of smiles and frowns. This was just stupid. Why would he do that? Zebo was right. OB must be psycho.

I grabbed another volume and saw OB's focus had changed. Now he was obsessed with a girl. There were poems, no, more like song lyrics because there were chord letters written above them. Looked like a lot of lost love stuff.

"Listen to this," I said. "Bring me down, down, to your level, open the gates of hell. Wrap me in lava if not your arms . . ."

"What shit!" Zebo said.

"This, too," Henry said. He had a pile of paper now, its layers crinkled like baklava.

"There's only one place to put shit," Zebo said. He scooped up the papers from the floor and ran across the hall to the bathroom. We followed. Zebo shredded a handful of notes into a toilet bowl and hit the flush handle with his foot.

"To the sewers!" he cheered.

"To the sewers!" we repeated, almost in unison. They tore notes until there were none, then helped me with the notebooks, ripping the pages from the bindings until the metal spirals stretched and hummed, warm to the touch. When the toilets got sluggish, Henry broke into the janitor's closet, retrieving a plunger he wielded like a javelin, churning the water with suction. One of the freshman opened the door. Zebo growled and chased the kid out into the hall. When Zebo came back in, he had OB's bag of soaps.

"Time to clean up," he said. He turned the water on in all the lavatories and unwrapped a bar of soap.

"Excalibur, May 28," he said. He tossed the bar into the sink. It was round and white, etched with the outline of a castle. One by one they hit the porcelain, and the water that splashed off the bars onto the floor mingled with the papery swill from the overflowing toilets.

I leaned back against the wall. I had one more notebook. The tile was cool through my T-shirt. It felt like those big ceramic squares were my personal kryptonite, draining all the energy from my body, leaving me with a churning stomach and a light head. I slid down to the floor and sat with my legs stretched out in front of me, the notebook in my lap. I held it close to my eyes and tried to focus.

The top page had several titles written in. "The Fire Last Time," "Brand Identity," and "Blair's Kangaroo," were lightly crossed out. "One Bare Spot" was circled.

"It's funny what you grab in a fire," I read. "Instead of money or your winter coat, things that might mean safety or survival, your brain goes on some kind of autopilot, grabbing what at first may seem like random objects, which later prove to be more, much more. When John Blair escaped from his smoke-filled bedroom wrapped in the sheets from his bed, he carried his guitar case, an old backpack of notebooks from grade school, and a collection of hotel shampoos his father had brought home from business trips over the years. Those items would be all that would survive from his childhood, except Blair himself, of course. His house, his photos, his family, all gone. In their place was a scar across his chest, closely resembling the continent of Australia, a brand of sorts where the fire lashed out at the bare spot in his yellow cotton toga, that months in the burn unit could not erase."

My insides were swirling around now, like on the Tilt-a-Whirl, and I couldn't focus at all. I heard Zebo laugh and Henry singing in the hall. I leaned to the side to vomit, and when I wiped my mouth on my sleeve, my eyes came together on a pair of black sandals, then black pants, black shirt, and OB's face. He squatted next to me and held out his hand. I reached for it, but he brushed my hand away.

"My notebook," he said.

He blotted the front page on his pant leg and held the notebook against his chest. He hesitated, as if waiting for something to catch up with him, or to say something, but his eyes were focused elsewhere. He stood up.

"OB," I said.

He tilted his head ever so slightly and looked down under his curtain of bangs.

"I didn't . . ." I began. What I didn't know was how to finish that sentence. Didn't mean to? Didn't know about his past? Didn't think he'd mind?

Behind him the bathroom door slammed open into its opposite wall. From my vantage point on the tile I could see a familiar silhouette in the doorway. Candice put her hands on her hips and surveyed the room like Robert E. Lee at the Battle of the Crater. Her eyes lit on me.

"Brilliant," she said. "Just brilliant."

Linda H. Heuring

UNTIL THERE'S NOT

Roger navigates the three metal steps into the train with his hands full. The cardboard cup of coffee has a neckband to protect his hands, but it just makes the cup unstable. His briefcase leather is soft, scuffed, from three decades of transport. The rectangular handles, once stiff as belt buckles, droop into the shape of his folded fingers as if grafted onto his hand. He eases into the forward-facing bench where someone has scattered sections of today's *Trib*. Monday again. The acid reflux pill he chased with pomegranate juice this morning is not working.

He drops his briefcase on the seat opposite. The handles scrape the pointing finger of his left hand, leaving his Band-Aid in disarray. A black circle of a wound sits at the base of his thumb, and another is centered on the back of his hand. The Band-Aid hangs by a thread of adhesive off the tip of his fingernail. He touches the bandage with the edge of his cup, but he might as well be wearing boxing gloves. He feints with the cup as the train takes off. He hovers it over the seat with his briefcase, then waves past it, to the air above the seat beside him. God, no. He can't sit it on the seat. Does he need to give that fucker Ravi any more ammunition by arriving with a butt load of coffee on the back of his pants? No, he leans over and balances the cardboard in the moon-shaped circle between his dress shoes. He wiggles the Band-Aid around, but it's not going to stay. He knows that. It's like a triangular hat made of newspaper that won't last. His hands tremble. He retrieves his cup with both hands and takes a sip as the train slows. He grabs his briefcase, and the Band-Aid flips up like the lid on a Zippo.

One stop, he's off. A short trip on public transportation, but he doesn't want to park his geezer car, the Mercury Grand Marquis he's babied for years, next to these kids' BMWs and Scions. The Band-Aid is a war wound in a battle with the Merc; he cut the fingertip and mashed his hand when he changed the wiper blades Saturday. Damned skin's as thin as those tasteless rice noodles Peking House delivered by mistake. Good wiper blades improve visibility, but these kids, boys mostly, didn't change wiper blades. They changed cars. Or didn't. Ran them into the ground and got another. Always more to come. He didn't blame them. He must have thought that once, too. Always more to come—until there's not.

He's the third to arrive. Some won't come in till nearly noon. He's best in the a.m., so he gets in around 7. He makes room in the communal fridge for his lunch, careful not to get too close to the round object growing what looks like chia pet hair. He's lost 25 pounds and 70 points on his cholesterol by changing to a Mediterranean diet. Mostly vegetables and fish. The boys are curious. They watch him unpack his little plastic containers every day at lunch. They all eat at their desks. The kids grab something from the machine. Or share delivery pizza. Four days in a row pizza from a soggy box. His stomach hurts just thinking about it. They hoover up his leftovers.

"You going to eat that biscotti, Roger?"

"What about that apple, Roger? You just going to let it sit there till it rots, or can I take it off your hands?"

Shove anything in their mouths, these boys. Until they can't.

He walks the cube-aisle past Sonya, the only woman on the project, her head clamped between a set of honest-to-god headphones, not the earbuds the boys all wear. He points a thumb in the air, a question. She smiles and wags him a thumbs up. Evidently she got up the nerve to read some of her poetry at an open mike downtown last night. She turns back to her monitors and flexes her toes to make a bright orange flip flop slap her sole as she concentrates. She keeps to herself, like he does, an outsider based on sex and style. If he had to bet on talent, he'd bet on her. Not that the boys weren't brilliant. He'd give them all that. They might not be the IBM-suit-and-tie professionals he'd started out with, but he'd learned not to let the desks cluttered with action figures and pinups of video game characters and brochures on $100,000 cars color his judgement. Creativity knows no package.

Roger boots up his laptop. The kids showed him the value of multiple monitors. He plugs in, and his screens flash gray, then blue. A shadow falls across his desk. A break in the fluorescent glare, a twitch in the fabric of the universe. Ravi.

"There is a call at 8:30," Ravi says. He grips an empty cardboard file box through one handle.

Roger nods. He knows there's a call. There's one every Monday at 8:30. Just the idea of Mumbai time being a half hour different than the entire rest of the world pisses him off. The call is on his calendar, synced with his iPhone, his computer, his brain.

"I need you to fill me in beforehand," Ravi says.

"The PowerPoint's on the server."

"IrREgardless," Ravi says, his emphasis on the second syllable. "Walk me through it."

It's irreGARDless, Roger thinks. Half the time he has to translate, shift the accent around in his head until he finds the word Ravi butchered. Ravi's got an MBA from Princeton, but he hasn't learned how to pronounce the words he uses. Hasn't learned? Doesn't bother? Maybe he's a leader in the evolution of the English language? TRENDING: accent marks shifting! Some twat or twit will tweet that eventually. Just because Roger doesn't use Twitter doesn't mean he is ignorant of the process. Roger is a process man at heart.

Roger types in his password and his Band-Aid spins. Ravi winces. That's a story about Ravi he wasn't sure was true. Rumor has it that Ravi once saw his son with a nosebleed and fainted dead away. Roger pulls up the presentation on his larger monitor and clicks through the slides.

Each time Roger looks up, Ravi is nodding his head. Even if he hadn't sat through the workshop on "cross cultural issues" human resources rotated all the consultants through, he'd have learned by now that Ravi's head-nodding is no more a sign of agreement than the White Sox bobble-head on his grandson's low-rider dash. The whole training session was about how the Americans had to adjust. Realize there was a tendency to say "yes" without working through the consequences. And no respect for time. Well, that's not exactly what the trainer said, but that was the gist to Roger.

"We in the United States are in a monochronic culture," she said. "We see time as linear, and we concentrate on one thing at a time, even though some of us do have a penchant for multi-tasking." The class had chuckled at that.

"However, the culture in India is polychronic. They see time as cyclical. There are lots of interruptions and many things going on at once. An objective is just a suggestion, not a deadline like it would be in a monochronic culture. What's important is the relationships, not the output. Hence, the disconnect when working offshore."

For Roger, though, this wasn't offshore. It was here, in Chicago, on the shores of the great Lake Michigan, and all this adapting was shredding his stomach lining like paper. Roger's job was one of go-between, making sure the client who wanted the software developed got what it wanted and making sure the developers, who were actually programming, knew what was required. A translator of sorts between business speak and cyberspeak. So when Ravi tells the client, "yes, yes, yes," and the programmers explain there's no fucking way, Roger becomes the monkey in the middle. Until he isn't.

Ravi puts the empty file box on the desk. Roger's name is scrawled on the side in thick black Sharpie ink.

"For your things," Ravi said.

"My things?"

"To take home. We no longer need you."

"Just like that?" Roger says. It is so like Ravi. Did he learn this at Princeton or in some human resources workshop on letting people go?

Roger stands up and watches as Ravi steps back. It hits him for the first time that Ravi might be afraid of him. Not professionally, or intellectually, but physically.

He steps closer to Ravi, invading his personal space, something Ravi frequently does to him. "And there's a reason, I presume?"

Ravi steps back again. Roger nods his head. It's true, he thinks. Now he loosens his neck and lets his head bob, then roll.

"You're not friendly."

"I'm not WHAT?" Roger stops nodding and laughs. Out loud. He realizes it's out of character. He tends to have individual conversations, quiet discussions, unless he is presenting. He focuses on the task at hand. Definitely monochronic.

The cubicles all open to the center, and Roger realizes the office has filled up but is strangely quiet. He shakes his head from side to side, not a cultural affectation but a universal signal that things are not all right. His coffee rises up his esophagus, and he holds a fist to his chest and walks into the lunchroom. He drinks a glass of water and the burning eases somewhat.

He retrieves his lunch and packs up his briefcase. He pushes the file box aside, and it rattles. Inside there's a metal button, pink lettering on a white background, which he recognizes. It's been stuck to the wall of Sonya's cubicle since the day she arrived. He knows the line is from *A Midsummer Night's Dream*: "Though she be but little she is fierce." He looks over at Sonya. She smiles and gives him the y-pantomine for "call me." He turns the button over to see her number on the back.

He zips up his briefcase as a red ball of fur sails into the box, followed by a chirpy electronic "ouch." A stuffed and angry bird has landed. Then a Green Hornet action figure. A can of gummy bears. A double-pack of Snickers bars. A rubber band shaped like a Humvee. A banana. One of these boys bought fruit?

Roger nods to the team as he picks up his briefcase and cradles the box under one arm. When he punches the elevator button he leaves behind a smear of red. His Band-Aid is gone, and he's opened his wiper wound. As the doors close, he sees Ravi headed his way, and in the seconds of hesitation before the wheels turn the cables to take him downstairs, Roger hears a thud. He smiles. A blood rumor is just a rumor, until it's not.

A WOMAN WALKED INTO THE BAR

A woman walked into the bar.

A woman with a stained wrist-to-bicep cast walked into the bar.

A woman walked into the Red Fox bar holding up a ragged forearm cast like one of Wonder Woman's indestructible bracelets, and with her good hand she shredded a pink rose into Richie's half-full beer mug.

She walked back to the door I'd propped open to air out the place, and all the regulars moved down a stool. She picked another rose from the bush that grew in that crack of dirt between the sidewalk and the brick and stuck this one behind her ear, thorns and all. I thought that should hurt. She parked on an empty stool.

"Gin and tonic," she said.

Not many people ordered mixed drinks here. The Red Fox was a townie bar in a college town, and on a good night I made maybe a couple of rum and Cokes or a screwdriver. Mostly it was cheap, pale beer on tap. That was a good thing, because anything more exotic than that would send me to the *Mr. Boston Deluxe Official Bartender's Guide* I carried back and forth to work. The guide was a present from the mother of one of our friends after she spent the night in our apartment when her son was inducted into Phi Beta Kappa. He went out partying, and we entertained his mother. Go figure. I made a him a cake with runny icing. I have a photo of it somewhere. I have no photos of the Red Fox.

I mixed up the gin and tonic and sat it on the black lacquer surface in front of her. We didn't use cocktail napkins. Cocktail napkins were a luxury Scottie, the bar owner, didn't spring for. I have no idea whether he made a profit or not. I wasn't even allowed to count the money at the end of the night. I had to put it in a paper bag and bury it under a clean trash bag in the waste can under the bar. He counted it in the mornings, and when I relieved him for my evening shift he was meticulous about chastising me if the total on the cash register didn't match what was in the bag. It was a one-man bar, manned five out of seven nights by a skinny college senior, *moi*, who drew 25-cent mugs of beer, washed glasses, tossed frozen breaded mushrooms into the deep fryer, sliced questionable lunchmeat for sandwiches, waited tables, tended bar, and swept up at the end of the night. I couldn't even go to the bathroom without asking one of the regulars to keep an eye on things. When no one was there, I was tethered to that ancient expanse of oak and brass, the only thing of beauty in the place.

Rose, that's what I named her in my head, sat there mumbling. She'd look up once in a while to stare at Richie fishing petals out of his mug with two fingers he waggled like tweezers.

"That's a dollar," I told her.

148

She glared at me.

"The drink. It costs a dollar," I said.

"My money's gone," she said. She thumped her cast on the bar.

"Missing." Thump.

"Stole." Thump.

"I can't give you that for free," I said. Well, that wasn't quite true. She could get it for free, but I'd have to pay for it. I was still smarting from the week before when the owner took the price of a case of beer out of my paycheck because I let a brassy-haired woman walk out the door with it. She said he said for her to pick up the case of longnecks and deliver it to him. What was I thinking? I was thinking he told her to. After all, I'd seen them cozied up at the end of the bar. I thought they might be having a thing, but I was the one who got screwed. He said. She said. Way before "don't ask, don't tell" was about sexual preference.

Rose slumped against the bar and started to cry. Her boobs rambled around in her thin sack dress. She wove her free fingers into her platinum hair, ends and pieces sticking out like it was cut with pinking shears and no mirror. She didn't wipe her face or anything, just cried and let the tears fall wherever.

"Here." Richie pushed a damp dollar bill across the bar to me.

"You know her?" I said.

He shook his head, a warning. Not now.

Rose gulped her drink, kicked over a chair, and walked out.

The regulars moved back to their normal spots.

"You should call the cops," Harry, one of the regulars, said.

"For what? Richie paid."

"Trust me. She'll be back. Now she knows she can drink for free."

I pulled a clean mug from the chest freezer behind the bar, tilted it under the tap emblazoned with a golden eagle and watched Budweiser climb up the glass. I traded Richie for his empty, which I washed in the bar sink and plunked back in the freezer wet.

"So, who is she, anyway?"

Richie made a little pile of the wet rose petals in front of him and shifted on his bar stool.

A series of mugs were slid toward the back of the bar, and the regulars swiveled on their vinyl and chrome seats to point to Richie. Except for the guy who was closest to the door. He faced outside, a designated lookout. I stacked the empties in the sink and poured a new round.

Richie took a long draw on his beer and exhaled an equally long sigh. He worked maintenance at the University, and he most always had a story about something stupid the college kids had done, like take in a litter of abandoned puppies and raise them in the attic of Rogerts Hall. I didn't tell him that we had adopted one of the little border collie mixes. We named her Pearl after a Janice Joplin album.

"Annette Cartright," Richie began. "That's her name. Annette Cartright."

"Not one of the Cartrights the Arts Center is named after," I said.

I got a sharp look from Harry. A look like, *quiet kid, let him talk.* So I piped a 7-Up from the tank into a glass with ice and leaned my back against the cash register.

"She must of just picked me. I never had two words with her."

Richie lit a cigarette. Everyone waited.

"I heard she got that cast from a fight with the state

cops. She went after her old man with a butcher knife," Richie said. "He's out of the hospital now. She just missed his liver."

I gripped my glass a little tighter. "So what's she doing walking around? Not in jail."

"Her husband, he don't want to press charges. Wants her back. Says she didn't mean anything by it," Richie said.

"Fourteen stitches don't mean anything," Harry said. He shook his head. "I was you, I'd call the cops."

"She's not even here. I'll look like an idiot."

"Like they'd even come since she put one of them troopers in the hospital," Richie said. "Word is he's got a bad concussion. Some broken bones."

"Wouldn't you think she'd get jail time for that?"

Richie shrugged again. "Bail, maybe." He ran a finger through a ring of beer sweat.

I scanned their faces for signs of a smile, a sideways glance. They were a tight group, prone to collude on a practical joke—like the leggy rubber spider they left lurking under my bar rag, the tap ornaments switched while I manned the deep fryer in the back, that sort of thing. No hints of a ruse tonight.

I stuck a finger in the watch pocket of my Levi's to check for the emergency phone quarter. The dial on the phone behind the bar could spin until the cows came home and never connect. It was for incoming calls only, something the owner arranged with Ma Bell to get every last cent from the customers. No one could convince a gullible barkeep to let them use the phone if it didn't make calls. No, they'd have to spend a quarter a pop to use the pay phone by the door. The downside was the bartender had to stroll over to the pay phone to get help if trouble blew in. The number for the cops was on a slip of paper by the register. What if I couldn't remember it when the time came? I wrote the seven digits on the inside of my wrist in ball point.

By nine o'clock the foot traffic on the old brick sidewalk out front was pretty steady with frat boys and sorority sisters making their way to Top Hat, the bigger and relatively cleaner bar just around the corner. Top Hat had a new juke box packed with Grace Slick and Jethro Tull. The 45s here leaned toward tears-in-my-beer country tunes, and some nights Willie Nelson sounded downright hoarse after the umpteenth play of "Blue Eyes Crying in the Rain." Richie was often the culprit, six plays for a quarter, and every one of them a lament to the "saint of a woman" who kicked him from the marital bed to a Murphy bed in a plastic and orange shag efficiency. No wonder he preferred this smoky refuge.

The place started to clear out just after 10, everyone but Richie headed home to someone or something. He had just plunked in another quarter's worth of Willie and made a detour to the can when Rose came through the open door. She just didn't seem like an Annette to me. She deliberately scratched black marks into the linoleum with her overrun shoes. Then she made straight for the Wurlitzer and knocked it with her hip. She watched as Willy skipped to the end and was lifted back into the stacks by the mechanical arm. The arm swung to the first position, then back to pick up Willie again. When he began to sing, she smacked her cast on the jukebox. She turned toward me. Her thumb protruded from a hole in the cast that was ringed black with grime. She held it vertically, a hammer to the gun barrel of her pointing index finger. Pointing at me. She lowered her thumb, the hammer down, the imaginary bullet headed my way. She blew a puff of air over the tip of her index finger, replaced it in an imaginary holster, and walked out. I left my sanctuary behind the bar and dialed the police.

"You let us know if she comes back," the dispatcher said. She hung up.

I went back to the register, got another quarter, and dialed Scottie.

"What do you expect me to do? Come down there and babysit you?" he said. "She's just a crazy old coot. Figure it out."

Figure it out. Yeah, right. Figure out how to deal with crazy?

When Richie climbed back on his stool I was downing a shot of Jack Daniel's to stop the shakes Rose left me with.

"Drinking on the job?"

"It's allowed."

"Yeah, but you don't."

He was right. I preferred a tip to a customer's offer to buy me a drink. This was something else. I set the shot glass flat on the bar.

"She came back. Rose. Annette. While you were in the bathroom. She scared the crap out of me." I mimicked her gunshot pantomime.

"So I called the cops," I nodded at the pay phone, "and they aren't coming. No one's coming."

"They stay as far away from Nettie as they can," Richie said.

"I thought you didn't know her."

"Not her as she is now, but before."

"Before what?"

"Just before." Richie shrugged. Sipped his beer. Lit another cigarette. Closed his eyes and lip-synced to Willie.

I got it. It's not like he came here to see me. None of them did. They came for each other or their ghosts, or to hide from their ghosts. Or wives. I was barely a resident, a blip on the radar, a passing ship bound for other waters. I was at the Red Fox to serve them. Period. The bar and that woman, Rose, were not my problem.

What was my problem was finishing Richard Niebhur's *The Responsible Self* before class Monday. The light in the bar was shit for reading, but I tried anyway. I angled my book down by the fluorescent sink light under the bar, and I was a world away when Richie tapped his empty on the bar and made the light jiggle.

"Another."

When I put his change on the bar he slid an extra quarter my way for a tip and leaned back to light a cigarette. I rubbed my eyes to shift gears from student to bartender.

He wiped at the melting frost on the side of his glass with the back of his hand.

"Nettie was always a little different, you know? She'd be fine one minute and the next she'd get mean. Not just mouthy. She'd corner some girl in the bathroom and knock her down. For no reason. She'd get suspended for a few days, come back, and start all over again. One day she laid into me, kicked me in the stomach on the monkey bars. I hit the ground, and she was on me. Bloodied my nose. Ripped the pocket right off my shirt."

"What'd you do?"

"Nothing 'cause you're not supposed to hit a girl."

I shook my head.

"Someone got the playground teacher, and she hauled us to the office. We both got paddled for fighting. I'm still pissed about that. I didn't have nothing to do with her after that."

"What happened to her?"

"She left in junior high and never came back. Her brother told me once about all the medicines they put her on. Those shock treatments in France or Switzerland or somewhere none of us had been."

"So she *is* one of those Cartrights."

"The only one left now."

"How well did you know her?"

"Well enough."

"When did she come back?"

Richie shrugged.

"What's wrong with her? Is she manic-depressive? Schizoid?" I took *Introduction to Psychology* like everyone else, and when I wasn't diagnosing myself, I was diagnosing my friends.

Richie shoved his empty toward me and stood up.

"What is this, twenty fucking questions? If I could answer that I'd be some rich doctor instead of cleaning up after you college shits." He wiped his change off the bar, including the quarter he'd left for me. He hitched up his pants. The keys on his belt jingled as he left.

The Miller Lite clock said 11:00. Four hours until last call. Half-hour more to closing. I sat at the bar stool by the open door where the streetlamp produced a shaft of light and started to study again. I wasn't going to tend bar for the rest of my life. That's why I became a "college shit" in the first place.

It wasn't easy to concentrate. Every little noise, I'd look up. I nearly jumped off my stool when someone stopped in the doorway.

"You work here?" It was Roger, a guy from one of my classes.

"No, I just come here for the good lighting and the spilled beer."

He glanced at my book and groaned.

"I haven't finished it either. Think he'll notice?"

There were only five of us in Dr. Eigenbrodt's *God and Evil* class. He'd notice.

"You didn't happen to see a weird woman with a cast lurking around out there, did you?"

"No, why?" He held onto the door frame and looked the street up and down.

"She came in here earlier and threatened me. She's crazy."

"Hitler crazy or regular crazy?" Roger said.

I started to laugh, then caught myself and shrugged. Roger and I had come up with that in class last week. We made a distinction between truly evil people who happened to be crazy and those with mental illness.

"Hitler was pure evil, delusional," Roger said in class.

"But certifiable. Does being crazy give him a walk? He wasn't responsible for his actions because of his mental illness? Was the evil his mental illness and not his nature?" I said.

"So we have a line to cross between Hitler crazy and just plain crazy?" Roger said, and we laughed, using the line a dozen times before class was over. Tonight it wasn't so funny. Who was I to determine where Nettie Rose might stand relative to that line? I didn't even know her. I did know, though, that I was afraid of her, and I could use some company.

"You want to come in for a beer? On the house," I said. Not really on the house. More like "on me," but it was certainly worth a quarter to have someone else there.

Roger glanced behind him.

"A quick one. I'm waiting for my roommate to finish up next door."

I poured him a beer and put my emergency quarter in the till.

"Frosted mugs? Here?" he said.

"Our one claim to fame."

A shadow passed the street light, someone lurching toward campus.

"My roommate," Roger said, draining his mug. "Have to get him back to the dorm. Hard to believe someone's in worse shape than me."

When they staggered off, they brushed the rose bush. Petals fluttered onto the threshold. I bent to pick them up and saw the black marks Rose had left on the linoleum. Cleaning might be therapeutic.

I was on my hands and knees scrubbing the floor when two pair of sturdy black shoes walked in. The cops.

"You called about Nettie?" one of them said.

"Yeah." I looked at the clock. "About two hours ago."

"Guess she really is at the Shamrock," the other one said.

"You're here because you heard she's someplace else?" I stood up.

"Let us know if she comes back."

At three I shut down the taps and carried the trash to the alley through the back door. I turned off the fryer and stuffed my book in my bag. I unplugged the juke box, set the chairs on the tables, and stuffed the money under the trash bag as usual. I perched on a stool and watched the clock.

At 3:20 Nettie came back in. I edged around behind the bar. She stood between stools and ordered a gin and tonic.

"I'm sorry, Nettie," I said. I know my voice was broken. I pointed at the clock. "After three. It's against the law."

She looked around. The place was empty. Who would know?

"Gin and tonic," she said.

"I can't serve anything after three, Nettie," I said, hoping that calling her by name would let her know I was friendly. Sorry. Sympatico. "They'll yank my license, Nettie."

She took two steps back and glared at me.

"I don't know you." She made her broken arm into a gun again.

"Don't," she said. She stabbed the pointing-finger-barrel at me.

"Say." Stab.

"My." Stab.

"Name!" She let the hammer down with a psheew.

She turned on her heel and came around behind the bar toward me. I ran out the other side and headed for the phone. My fingers reached for the emergency quarter that was no longer there, and Nettie reached for a bottle.

She upended a fifth of Beefeater over her mouth and drank from the metal pouring spout. She kept a tight fist on the bottle's neck and wiped her mouth on her arm. She glared at me and ran her cast along the glass shelf behind the bar, making missiles of the paltry selection of bottled booze Scottie kept on hand. Broken fifths of bourbon and vodka mixed with half liters of rum on the bar and on the floor. She ripped the bar phone from the wall and smashed it against the back mirror, which cracked.

I hovered in the doorway by the pay phone, straddling the threshold. I had strict orders not to leave the bar, but how could a reasonable person expect me to stay?

Nettie found the bar glasses and hurled one in my general direction. It smashed against the door frame and sent shards into my cheek, close to my eye. I ran.

The Top Hat was closed, like I should have been by now. I pounded on the front window until the bartender let me in. He dabbed at the cut on my cheek with a white bar napkin while I called the police. Then I called Scottie.

"You know what time it is?" Scottie said. "Who the fuck is this?"

"Alice," I said. "That woman . . ."

"I told you to handle that crazy bitch. Why aren't you closed?"

"You need to come down here. I can't do this." Richie was right. I was a college shit, ill-prepared to deal with something like this.

"If I have to come down there, I sure as hell don't need you. You're fucking fired."

The bartender, Craig it turns out, made me an ice pack from a clean bar towel. He locked up and waited with me outside the Red Fox while Nettie Rose wore herself out smashing and heaving everything that wasn't nailed down. When she left, she didn't even glance at the two of us leaning against the side of the building. She loped off down the middle of the street.

The Red Fox smelled worse than a frat house after a party, what could have been smoky and sweet was cloying. I was afraid I'd throw up and add to the aromatic mix. I pressed a corner of the bar towel/icepack to my nose and mouth and waded into the mess. I found my book bag wedged between two booths. I stood against the open door until Scottie came. He paused for half a second, then pushed past me to get behind the bar. Glass crunched under his shoes. He bent down under the sink, and when he stood he had one hand down the back of his pants. He looked me in the eye. The money bag. He saw. I saw.

A woman walked out of the bar.

A woman with a gash in her cheek walked out of the bar.

A Woman Walked into the Bar

A woman with a gash in her cheek walked out of the Red Fox bar holding a book bag to her chest like a Viking shield, picked a pink rose off the bush near the door and stuck it behind her ear. It didn't hurt as much as I thought it would.

Linda H. Heuring

BREAKING POINT

Mary Louise always said Jesus knew everything in advance. I don't know where she got that, like I don't know where she got off starving herself for so many years that she ended up in that wheelchair on my front stoop, abandoned like a kitten.

If Jesus knew it all, why didn't he clue me in? He and I didn't have that mind-meld He had with Mary Louise. What if I wasn't home? But I was. I was up to my elbows in bread dough when the doorbell rang. I turned the doorknob with a linen towel, and there she sat, drowning in cotton fleece.

"My God, Mary Louise? What are you doing here?" I looked past her. It was the typical Wednesday: trash cans at the curb, a lawn service trailer halfway blocking the cul de sac.

"That's for me to know and you to find out," I remember her saying, like Calvin in one of his essays on predestination, quoting God. But memory can play tricks on you, and if she had really said that, would I have brought her inside? Would I have hauled that heavy chair over the threshold and parked her at my kitchen counter while I shaped smooth, white, pliable dough into loaves that looked remarkably like her hairless scalp? Without the ears, of course. Who ever heard of bread with ears?

We sat on my screen porch that jutted out over the Savannah River. Mary Louise balanced a MacBook on her lap. The rising bread loaves sat in the sun next to us, straining at the cloth like breasts in a cotton blouse. Mary Louise's breasts were long gone, melted away like every other fat cell her body could burn for fuel.

"How did you get here?"

"Debra." Mary Louise flipped her hand in the air, dismissing her daughter, her only living relative. Even if the link wasn't biological.

"When is she coming back?" I said.

Mary Louise caressed the laptop's touch pad with her index finger. Her nails were short and lined.

"She's not." She tapped the pad. Click. Click again.

"Not what, Mary Louise?"

"Not coming back. Not ever. Good riddance. I don't need her and that pretty boy husband of hers telling me what to do. You know I can't tolerate the pretty boys."

I ignored her crack about my college boyfriend. She wasn't going to turn me into that insecure girl again.

"Debra drove ten hours and just left?"

Mary Louise squinted at the laptop screen.

"You need a shade for out here. There's glare on my screen," she said. She rubbed her hand over her scalp, and the loaves of bread quivered on the baking sheet.

"You're not planning to bake that," she said. "The smell makes me sick to my stomach."

I could bake the bread at my neighbor's. There the aroma would be welcome. But it was the principle of the thing. It was SO Mary Louise to just barge in. Barge in and take over. I liked my solitude, setting my own schedule. If I got in mind to bake lasagna at 2 a.m., no one could ask me if I was insane. And if I wanted to spend my afternoon sitting on this screened porch staring at the Savannah, well that was also my choice. She made choices, too. She'd chosen not to eat. At least in the beginning it was a choice.

"Aren't you taking anything?" I said.

"Any what?"

"Anything to keep the food down."

Mary Louise laughed and coughed into a tissue that appeared from up her sleeve.

"Nothing to keep down. Not for days," she said. Her finger joints moved underneath her skin. She coughed again and pressed a nearly-empty sleeve to her chest. "I think that was another rib."

"A rib? My God!" I reached for her. What did you do with broken ribs? Tape them?

"Nothing to do. It won't heal. If you tape it something else will break."

Had she read my mind? No, we probably learned to tape ribs in a shared first aid class. She was strong then, muscular. She played field hockey. She danced. She ate real food.

Mary Louise tossed her dirty tissue onto a green square of my checkerboard porch floor and put her hand on mine. It was dry and cold, like one of Anne Rice's vampires, swooping in to suck the life out of me. My fingers were pudgy and soft, middle-aged hands. They always surprise me, these signs of middle age. On a good day a twenty-five year-old looks back at me in the mirror, confident and full of promise. On a bad day, and don't ask me why I'm always surprised by this, on a bad day I see my grandmother looking back at me. On those days it takes everything I have not to crawl back into bed.

"Are you in pain?" I touched her forehead as if to brush away a lock of hair.

She shook off my hand and dug around in a flat red bag attached to the inside of her wheelchair. She pulled out some crumpled foil and a wood and brass pipe with a small bowl.

"I can't believe you still have that," I said. "And use it."

"Get me a light," she said, poking a bit of hashish into the bowl. "Debra took my lighter."

"How do you even get the stuff?"

"I have my ways." Mary Louise pointed the pipe at me like our old sociology professor used to, poking the stem in the air toward a student from whom he expected an intelligent comment.

"You," she said, "get me a light."

I broke the first match I tried to strike, a long skinny fireplace match from who knew how many Christmases ago.

"You always were clumsy," Mary Louise said. "From the very first."

It was a word smack across my face. Mary Louise's cuts were not scalpel fine and subtle, but jagged and angry like a dull serrated knife. She started the day I arrived in the freshman dorm with my two long braids and cut-off overalls. She sat on her bed and waved her hand toward one-quarter of our dorm room.

"Your side," she had said, trailing a stream of cigarette smoke from the fag held between her finger and her thumb. She paused to make sure I was watching.

"My side," she said. She pointed to the rest of the room. "Questions?"

She looked at me with her eyes half-closed, a James Dean look I attributed to the long curl of smoke twisting toward her straight-cut bangs. I hoped we could sort it out later. After all, I'd just arrived. If I was a big fish in a consolidated high school, Mary Louise was a whale. The bio the university sent me beforehand said she was a National Merit Scholar and math prodigy from Chicago. I was hoping she wouldn't see me as too much of a hick.

"You always dress like Heidi, the goat girl?" she said.

So much for first impressions. I tripped on the rug and bumped into the edge of my desk.

"Walk much?" she said.

If I'd talked back to her then things might have been different later, but I wasn't clued in to the politics of dealing with girlfriends. They always seemed one step ahead of me, even physically. A junior high classmate whose chest prominently poked out underneath her bra once pulled my T-shirt away from my neck and looked at my bare chest.

"You'll be swelling up soon," she said with some authority. I grabbed my shirt neck and went into the house.

Girls were too intimate, too intimidating, too much, like my neighbor's Siamese cats, making baby crying noises, slicking down their fur, purring one minute then clawing the skin off the back of your hand the next. Boys, I understood. With boys you knew what was what. And once they said what they had to say, it was over. With Mary Louise it was never over.

Mary Louise took a big draw on her pipe and rolled her head against the back of the chair, holding the smoke in for so long I half-wondered if she was still alive. She tried to hand me the pipe.

"You kidding? It's been years," I said.

"Could be that's your problem," Mary Louise said.

"You think?" I looked through the porch screen to the river below, scanning the water for passing boaters who might smell something. Mary Louise took another drag.

"The Angela I remember was reckless. A murderer." She let that hang in the air. "Of the innocent, of course."

She narrowed her eyes and attempted that James Dean look again, but the predatory stare had lost its muscle. I thought of children needing sponsors for a dime a day.

"The past is past," I said. Even my quiet voice seemed to echo across into South Carolina.

"Is it now? Says the one of us with a future."

"And that's my fault?" I stood up. "I've got to see to the bread."

The loaves were more than ready to bake. If I wasn't careful they'd collapse, expanded beyond their capacity to sustain themselves. I slid them into the oven, gave them a quick spritz with water to make crusty crust, and turned on the timer.

I put two glasses and a bucket of ice on a tray with a bottle of Jack Daniel's. The bottle was decorated with a ribbon and a congrats card from my agent to celebrate the bourbon cookbook I'd finished when, last year? The year before? I drank mostly wine now, but it didn't seem like a wine kind of day. Besides, Mary Louise had always liked bourbon.

Mary Louise had drawn her legs up into the wheelchair under an afghan she took off the back of the wicker love seat. Her eyes were closed.

This screen porch was my favorite place, an extension of the kitchen, and it hung out over the river on some kind of supports that the home inspector told me were "very well planted," whatever that meant. From here I could go out a side door to another deck that wrapped around past my bedroom with its wall of glass doors that I slid open at night to catch the breeze. The inspector told me the wrap-around needed more uprights to be safe for children, but I neither had nor expected any.

I sipped the coolest top layer of bourbon and watched the river. I liked its permanence. A few early leaves floated on the surface, headed for the rapids just down river, where they would swirl around boulders and stuck logs on a futile trek toward the ocean.

Over in her chair, Mary Louise extended her palm like a little tray for a glass. Waiting for me to notice.

"I thought you were asleep." I fixed her drink.

"I still have nightmares, you know," she said.

"Nightmares?"

"Nightmares. Are you deaf?" She opened her eyes and shifted in her chair. "I know I'll see hell, and the spot right next to me?" She pointed at the floor. "Got your name all over it."

I touched my tongue to an ice cube. It was slick.

"I can see it, pale as pale can be. And bloody," she said. "God, there was a lot of blood."

Oh, I remembered the blood all right. It made red streams in the hexagons of grout around the white floor tiles, following the lines like Pac Man creatures, but Pac Man hadn't been created yet. I had stood shivering, one leg inside the claw-footed bathtub and the other feeling the tile floor, unable to will one leg to join the other, cramping and crying and praying to God this would just be over. Mary Louise had half-carried me to the hospital.

My doctor saw a rejected IUD he'd inserted only that morning. Mary Louise saw the fetus I'd delivered on the tile.

Safer than a coat hanger, the IUD.

I refilled my glass.

"We've been through this before," I said. "Borrowing urine isn't a cardinal sin."

"I knew what you were doing and so did you. Cheating the test. He'd have never put it in if you were pregnant."

The oven buzzer sounded two long beeps.

"What was I supposed to do, Mary Louise?"

"I told you what to do," she said. "You and me. We'd raise it together."

The buzzer went off again. I could just see my bread burning around the edges. I slammed my drink down on the glass top of the end table and went inside. The bread thumped hollow on the bottom. It was dark brown, but not burnt. I slid the loaves onto the cooling rack.

It felt like my heart was somewhere in the back of my throat, pumping blood straight into my ears and eyeballs. I knew better than to drink with Mary Louise, so why did I? My blood pressure was up. Sometimes it got so bad I could hardly see. Now, though, I could see Mary Louise on the porch pounding the ashes out of her pipe into the dirt of a potted hibiscus. She refilled her pipe and struck the match herself. She always was capable, Mary Louise.

What possessed me two years ago, after decades of silence, to agree to connect with her on a social network, I can't tell you. I must have seen my college years through a prism, a retina-burning white light refracted into a rainbow of memories. Rainbows and unicorns and all things fanciful. And false.

We got together on neutral ground, a restaurant near a West Virginia rest stop. Mary Louise was recently widowed, her twenty-five year relationship with Kathryn ended by a car wreck. Kathryn had carried their daughter, Debra. Mary Louise barely touched her meal, but I wasn't that hungry, either. There was so much to say.

"Remember that night I found you asleep on the fire escape? You had marks on your cheek from using your tennis shoes as a pillow!" She laughed and sipped some water with a squeeze of lemon.

"There was the time we stole Pittman's coffee mug," I said. "It was like the Spanish inquisition. I know that's why I got a 'C' in Intro to Psych."

We were like kids again, lobbing shared stories across the formica table while our salads warmed and then were carried away by a waitress who just shook her head at our animated reunion. It would be another year before I knew Mary Louise's bones were dissolving like a chicken leg in a glass of soda pop. I was almost convinced our relationship had been a healthy one, two liberated girls negotiating our way into womanhood. But thirty years is a long time, and our relationship was like her bones, just way too many holes to patch up. What was I supposed to do with her now?

Steam hovered over the thick slices of bread I carried out onto the porch on a plate with hearty chunks of longhorn cheese. Mary Louise gagged at the smell and coughed into yet another tissue. I ate alone, making open-faced cheese sandwiches, which I washed down with bourbon. Bread was one of my specialties and one of my comfort foods. I could eat a whole loaf, and just looking at Mary Louise made me want to. She had her laptop open again, her fingers busy.

"You'll get fat, you know," she said, not looking up from the screen. "You've always leaned to the chunky side."

Chunky. She had loved calling me that and watched me gain and lose fifteen pounds twice a year for four years. She'd wear my "skinny" clothes without asking.

"Can't let these jeans go to waste," she told me one night, rubbing her cigarette ash into the denim instead of reaching for an ashtray. "You'll never squeeze your chunky ass in them again." I left the room in tears and ate nothing but lettuce for a week.

Sometimes she'd materialize behind me at the mirror and brush her hand across my rear or reach around and cup a breast as if testing its weight.

"This doesn't bother you, does it," she'd murmur, as I trembled there in my reflection, afraid to look up, afraid to move, afraid to appear uncool or intolerant or anti-feminist.

"You might want to think about losing a few pounds there, Angela," she'd say, finding a roll of fat to pinch. I explained away the bruises to my boyfriends and to myself. Clumsy, I could handle. Victim, I could not.

I cut another slice of cheese and piled it on a chunk of bread, not so much hungry as defiant.

"One would think someone in your position, Mary Louise, would have learned not to be so obsessed with weight."

"Like someone who cooks for a living would understand," she said.

"I write recipe books, Mary Louise. I've explained that before."

"Cooks for a living. Maybe you could work in a school cafeteria, opening those big cans of pork and beans." Her hands paused over the keys, like a concert pianist caught by a still photographer. She knew I hated working in the cafeteria in college. I cleaned trays, mopped floors, and stuck my hands in iodine water to sterilize glasses. We all wore jeans and T-shirts, the scholarship kids and the privileged, but the line of demarcation became very clear when we became the help.

Mary Louise snapped her laptop shut and wheeled over to me. "I need a refill."

"You sure this is a good idea?"

Mary Louise shook her head at me, like I was an ignorant child. She sucked in an ice cube and rolled it around her mouth before dropping it back into the glass. Bourbon splashed on her chin and stayed there. The drop glistened in the sun that was falling below the tree tops now, and the rays were split by the trunks of the Georgia pines on the riverbank. I fixed her drink.

I wiped the bread crumbs from my lap and looked out over the water. Maybe she would wear herself out and I could call Debra. I wasn't going to play Nurse Angela the rest of my life. Or hers. She closed her eyes again, and her head leaned to the side. I uncrossed my legs. My knees were stiff. I took two steps toward the phone and Mary Louise was awake.

"Have you thought about how you want to die?" she said.

"Not really. Frankly, I spend more time figuring out how not to."

"I'm thinking the Indians had the right idea," she said.

"India Indians or American Indians?"

"Native Americans, you fool. The ancient ones knew when the time came to die. They'd give away their possessions and wander off into the woods to die alone. So they wouldn't be a burden. Spend the last bit talking to the spirits."

"My brother's dog went missing right before she died," I said. "He found her in a little nest made out of tromped down grass like a crop circle. She was just laying there in the middle, all peaceful and dead with not a mark on her."

"At his house?"

"In the field across the street on his father-in-law's land. The dog roamed it all."

"That's what I'm talking about. I think cats do that, too. Find a place to die away from the family." She coughed again and wheeled over to the hibiscus. She pulled out her pipe.

"So, if you could choose how to die, how would you do it?" she said.

"Looks to me like you've already chosen starvation. That or to OD on hash and take my hibiscus with you."

"You can't OD on hash, and anyway, I wasn't talking about me. I asked you. In some *Thelma and Louise* scenario, whooping it up and driving right off a cliff?"

"I don't think I'm really the whooping it up type, Mary Louise."

"You used to be, so it's still in there somewhere. Covered over by layers of fat, most likely."

I placed one arm over my stomach, a reflex, then reached for another piece of bread.

"That wild child is long gone, Mary Louise. Long gone." But she was right. I had been just the type, a daring girl who gained confidence as our freshman year ran on. Parties. Drinking. Climbing into a locked athletic field at midnight to stretch out on the top row of the bleachers and see the stars. Playing with boys so different from those I went to high school with, boys who didn't see me as the freakish brainy one but as a girl to impress, to date, to touch. Oh, how I loved to be touched.

It was Mary Louise, for all her insults, her prodding, who showed me the ropes. Boiled water for instant coffee at 2 a.m. to keep my fingers moving across the typewriter keys to finish a psychology paper for a professor I hated.

Tutored me in math. Loaned me her best black turtleneck for a date with a fraternity guy. Made macrame earrings for my birthday. When I lurched into the room in the middle of the night, she held a trash can for me, a wet washcloth to my forehead, calling me a stupid bitch the whole time. The wild child. But that ended junior year when I met Damian.

"I left her behind even before we graduated, if you remember," I said.

"Because you let one guy suck all the life out of you. It was *Taming of the Shrew* all over again."

"Leave Damian out of this."

Mary Louise started coughing, gripping the edge of her wheelchair with one hand, holding her ribs with the other.

"He stole your spirit," she said.

"He stole nothing," I said. Damian, my shy troubled poet.

"Oh, no? You let him take your future. You're still mooning over him. Thirty years and you're not over him. His picture's even on your wall."

It was. I had decorated the living-room around the huge black and white print. Damian was sprawled in a chair, bare feet poking out of bell bottoms, a leather notebook open in his lap. He had been reading aloud, while I waltzed around taking random photos for class—candles and curtain rods and impromptu still lifes of the toiletries on his dresser.

"Keep reading," I told him. "Don't mind me."

But he put his poetry notebook down and turned his dark eyes on me like I was the only woman on earth. I pushed the shutter button down. Later, in the darkroom, when his image appeared under the liquid bath of chemicals, I thought I had captured his soul.

"You never did know what he meant to me," I said.

It was on a Thursday that I saw the police car in his yard. At the top of the stairs an officer blocked my path. Beyond him I saw bits of the room. A fragment of electrical cord. Ripped chapbooks. An overturned desk chair.

"But I'm his girlfriend," I said.

"You Angela?" he said. "There's a note."

The stationery was brown. Damian's tightly-printed capital letters in black ink. Six words: *How could you choose without me?*

I leaned against the wall and slid down to sit on the top step. A police radio squawked, a woman's official but soothing voice, enunciating, like a poet on stage at a coffeehouse. Two guys with a stretcher stepped over me.

Choose? My abortion was two years ago. I hadn't even met Damian.

The officer stared at me. I swallowed. I shook my head.

He held out his hand for the letter, pulled the door to, and followed the stretcher.

I sat there, fingering a blunt nailhead working its way loose from the riser. I sat until my rear end was as numb as my head, until Mary Louise led me by the hand across campus and into her bed.

Mary Louise refilled her pipe.

"See? Still mooning. Over something that was meant to be. Part of the plan."

"Who's plan?" It took my eyes a bit to focus on her now. The bread and the bourbon were making sugar in my system. "What the hell are you talking about, Mary Louise?"

"God's plan. Do you think it was coincidence we hooked up after all these years?"

All the nights we'd stayed up arguing philosophy with our floor mates, sprawled over thin cotton bedspreads from

India, the air thick with cigarette smoke and incense. Mary Louise's premise was that everything was already decided for us. God had a plan for our entire lives, not just a plan for what we would become, but down to the details. For someone the church had rejected so absolutely, she and God were certainly cozy.

"So why do you study at all, Mary Louise, if everything's decided? If your grades are already set, why bother?" someone had challenged her.

"It's predestined that I DO study and get the grades I get," she had retorted. "I don't have any choice but to study."

"Funny you should bring up choice," I said.

"Or murder." She glared at me, a you-don't-want-to-go-there look. I rolled over and lit a fresh cigarette.

"Okay, we'll use your word. Murder. Say someone reaches their breaking point. Like that woman who set the bed on fire while her husband was sleeping. So she takes his shit for years, and then one day she just snaps. Kills him. If what you believe is true, then there's no breaking point when your perception shifts and you pull the trigger or dive off the bridge or strike the match. It's more the end of a process. The culmination of a destiny determined when sperm penetrates egg and says, 'Honey, I'm home.'"

"At conception?" someone asked.

Mary Louise gave her the James Dean.

She tried giving it to me again, knocking her pipe against the chrome of her wheelchair.

"Do you, Angela?" she repeated.

"What?" I had no patience with this woman on my porch, dragging up mud from our past like a dredging barge. "What!"

"Do you think it's coincidence that I looked you up after all those years?"

175

"No telling, Mary Louise. I can tell you, though, I'm fixing to be sorry I answered." I knew I was crossing a line, a line between drunk and sober that I usually passed without recognition.

"No more coincidence than what happened to your precious Damian."

"You're saying God killed Damian?" I stood over her wheelchair.

She tilted her head up and blew a mouthful of sweet smoke into my face.

"I'm saying God saw what you were doing, holed up in some room for days at a time screwing and reading poetry. I'm saying that wasn't God's plan for you, and he got you back on track. He liberated you."

"Liberated? Freed me to a life alone? Did he liberate you, too? So you could die from a disease based on vanity? Have you no mirrors?"

Mary Louise was coughing, not even bothering with a tissue, just coughing and retching dry heaves into her empty hand. I grabbed the rubber grips on the handles of her chair and pushed her through the screen porch door onto the open deck. The river swirled beneath us. I turned her wheelchair toward the sliding glass door. I yanked her to her feet, and I thought I heard the crunch of bone. Mary Louise didn't make a sound. I held her chin in my hand and pointed to the glass. The two of us were reflected there in the grey blue light of the last of the sun on the river, me in my cargo shorts and tank top, as thick at the waist as everywhere else, and Mary Louise, a stick puppet in sweats.

"Look at yourself," I screamed at her, jabbing at the glass with my finger. "Just look at what you've done to yourself! For what?"

"For you," she said into the quiet. "And now, now

God has brought us back together. I knew he would."

Years reeled in my head, fast forwarding in black and white with a little red thrown in: Mary Louise pulling me away from the herd like a wolf after a sheep, lighting a candle for my aborted fetus, beating me with her voice, bruising me with her fingers. Mary Louise in a corner of the library whispering at Damian. Mary Louise pressing against my cold, numb body under the covers, kissing the tears from my cheeks, my neck, while Damian lay wrapped in a sheet on a porcelain table. God's will, indeed.

It was like sunset on the ocean. One minute the sun was a colossal red ball on the horizon and in the snap of a finger, we were plunged into darkness. One minute I held Mary Louise by the neck of her sweatshirt, and the next, she was gone. How could a body with bones as holey as a loaf of ciabbata bread sink so quickly?

∞

It's spring now. The drought is official. The water level at the reservoir that feeds the Savannah is at a record low. They've shut off the flow of water to the river to save the turbines, and the river narrows and shallows as she's pulled toward the sea. Downstream, when the angle is just right, I can see the glint of sunlight on chrome, a thin metal wheel on its side, spinning with the current, its spokes nearly invisible from rust. Who'd have thought the river would ever fall this low? Perhaps it was just another part of the plan Mary Louise and God cooked up. If so, he's not talking. At least not to me.

WHAT LIZA SAW

The sun dawned so hot Sally could see heat rise from the aluminum window sills of Don's trailer. She felt no ownership of this wheeled metal box on blocks in the middle of a trailer park. No trees, no shade, just row after row of trailers with gravel driveways and patches of pale grass as beaten down as the women who tended them.

She sat on the couch, while two-year-old Mike ate dry cereal at the coffee table with his fingers. It was too hot for milk. Too hot to think. Might be cooler at the kitchen table, but she couldn't haul him into his booster seat. She had strict orders to lift nothing heavier than a bottle of milk. Mike ate with his left fist, the other in a death grip on her skirt. He was always attached to her somewhere. Even in this heat, he stuck to her like a tick.

Perhaps the old wives were right: it was her grief that marked this child and made him fearful. Or the vengeance of the Lord. Except for his father's black hair, Winnan's family couldn't claim Mike in the dark. He was her son through and through. Even so, Don was jealous. Maybe after this baby, Don's baby, was born, things would change.

She heard Don's morning stream hit the toilet. He never closed the door, even though she'd asked. Some example he set for Mike.

Don banged around in the bedroom. "Where's my damned . . . never mind. I found them." He leaned against the door frame to put on his canvas shoes.

"Boo!" he shouted at Mike, then threw his head back and laughed.

Mike overturned his bowl, tripped, and hit his head on the edge of the table. Sally folded him into her skirt as best she could.

"It's okay, Mikey, it's okay." She patted him on the back and rubbed his head. No blood, but there would be a lump. Mike wailed.

"God-damned sissy," Don said.

Mike cried even louder.

"Shut up, boy, before I give you something to cry about." He took a step toward Mike, and Sally stood up.

"He's allowed to cry when he's hurt."

"He don't know the meaning of hurt." Don grabbed for the boy, but Mike buried his head up the back of Sally's skirt, and Don got only air. The man stepped back and swung again, connecting with Sally this time, his open palm as big as a paperback book when it smacked against her side.

Sally clutched her ribs with one hand and searched for Mike behind her back with the other. Her blouse fell open.

Don grabbed a swollen breast and twisted.

"And look at this! I don't get any of this." His voice was nearly a shriek. She bent over in pain.

Don was crossing the line. His voice got higher like

this before it dropped an octave and slipped into the danger zone. She had to tread carefully now. She reached out and stroked Don's arm as she pulled herself upright.

"You know I want to, sweetie, but you know what the doctor said. We don't want anything to happen to this baby. Our baby. Your baby."

"It was a good screwin' that made him, a little screwin's not gonna hurt him now." Don pushed her against the wall. She could feel him hard against her belly, his chest muscles, the bones of his hips.

"Besides, nothing says this one's really mine."

"Oh, he's yours all right." As she said it, Sally wished she'd swallowed the words.

Don smacked her in the face. Her right eye blurred, and she tasted blood. Mike whimpered, and she pried her son's hand from her skirt and shoved him behind the couch. Don punched her in the stomach then knocked her to the ground, a new low, even for him, she thought as she fell. She tried to block his kicks with her hands, but she couldn't completely protect this baby from his blows. She lay still and waited for Don to calm down. He always did. He wouldn't be sorry for a while yet, but he would calm down. With her one clear eye she watched him sink into his recliner and put his head in his hands. After a while he spoke, his words extensions of his fists.

"Why do you do this to me? I take you in when you're fixing to drop one, and I aim at being a good dad and what do I get? Some Bible college girl putting on airs. No wonder that husband of yours offed himself. He's gone. Gone! What you see here? That's what you get. Me, I just want what everybody else got. I want what I deserve."

She could smell him. No, taste him. Like iron. Not like the iron taste of the blood that coated the inside of her mouth and drained down the back of her throat, but hotter, more urgent, more dangerous, like the sizzling, still vibrating, sickening taste of the rail of a train track seconds after the L&N has passed. She felt her teeth with her tongue. The chair squeaked as he leaned forward. She opened her eyes. His canvas shoes were inches from her face. The shoes had turned yellow around the band. She could cover that with a little polish next time she washed them. She imagined herself shaking the bottle of white liquid, squeezing some onto the toe of his shoe, working it in, watching the yellow disappear. No, not disappear. Get covered over. The embarrassing stain would still be there underneath.

"I'm going to the river. It's too damn hot to stick around here."

Sally stayed put until she heard the car engine turn over and gravel ping against the aluminum trailer as he peeled out. She crawled toward the couch and propped herself against the battered paneling. Mike left his crevice of safety and curled up next to her.

"Baby." He patted her stomach with a sticky palm.

Sally smiled, and her lip split open again. She stopped the blood with the back of her hand.

She stretched and pushed on her back with her palms. Surely this wasn't the beginning of labor. She was still four weeks out, but early labor was what Doc Parker was so worried about. Stay off her feet. No lifting. No sex. Where would getting beat up fit on that scale? Doc said to get someone in to help. That wasn't going to happen. Don took any sign of need on her part personally, that he wasn't providing for her. Either that or he accused her of being too good to do what the other wives around here did, whatever that was. The other wives weren't very welcoming. High school friends all, they were bound together by sophomoric secrets they'd carry to the grave, secrets they'd never have shared with the virginal Sally. She escaped to college, while their lives were a continuation of high school, the same cliques and cars and rivalries. When Winnan got the church here, she'd followed the Lord's wishes, just like she'd tried to do every day since that kumbaya moment at church camp in junior high when she'd been saved, but that didn't mean she looked forward to living here again. Thankfully they'd treated her like a foreigner—the preacher's wife. Then she was the preacher's pregnant widow after Winnan, who never let a drop of alcohol touch his lips, was found dead in a farmer's pond inside their half-submerged car, surrounded by a case of floating empties.

Only Liza Burns had wanted to rekindle their friendship, sticking by her even after Winnan's fall from grace. Liza, who introduced her to Don. Don, who decided to spend the holiday waterskiing with friends and leave his hugely pregnant wife alone with a two-year-old in a stifling trailer with no phone and no car.

Sally's backache moved further down. The baby shifted.

"Great timing," she said to Mike. He tightened his grip on her blouse. She rummaged in the kitchen drawer for a pen and paper and a diaper pin.

"I am Mike," she printed in big letters. "Mommy's in labor. Please call . . ."

Who should she have them call? Who would come? Liza and her husband Matt were camping. There was really no one else. Don's mother? Not on your life.

"Please call for help," Sally wrote. She pinned the note to Mike's T-shirt with the diaper pin. Worse come to worse, she could point him to the trailer next door. She saw a running fan smashed up against their screen door.

She pushed the curtain away from the cereal box-sized bathroom window, turned on the cold tap, and filled the tub. She dropped her clothes to the floor piece by piece, and Mike gathered them up, like a retriever doing what he was bred to do. She stepped into the tub and slid down as far as she could. It must be close to 100 outside. Hotter in here. Even the cold water wasn't cold.

Her stomach was an island above the waterline, a collage of blues and blacks and spots of mottled yellow. Don had done a number on her this time. Her arms were bruised, and her breast was spotted purple with oval finger marks. What had she been thinking?

She thought that the Lord would provide for her, that's what. She thought this match came straight from heaven. She was kneeling by her bed, so swollen with Winnan's baby she wasn't sure she could get back up alone, praying for a sign, when Liza breezed in with a dinner invitation. Over a plate of Sunday chicken and a tall sweet tea Sally laughed for the first time in months. Don's charm, honed by his work as salesman at his father's Ford dealership, was salve to her wounds.

Don seemed oblivious to the talk about her late husband. Rumors of a scandal, a penchant for alcohol, another woman, circulated through the church and beyond. Don joked and wooed and handled her with kid gloves all through their ephemeral courtship. In a month they were married, she delivered Mike, and they moved into Don's rambling Victorian.

It was there she learned his charming smile came with an expiration date. When they disagreed on a spot for a bedroom chair, Don opened the window and tossed it outside. It smashed onto the sidewalk below.

"Problem solved," he said. Sally hoped it was just a

short term adjustment from so many years of bachelorhood, but that hope went the way of the bedroom chair, the glassware, and anything else Don could reach when life didn't deliver as expected. When Don's father died, Don wouldn't go to work. When Ford yanked the dealership, and the bank called the loans, they lost the house, too. The banker waited until the car was packed to padlock the door.

Don's mother financed the trailer with some cash that escaped the bankers. Sally scrubbed the stained linoleum and the rust-streaked bathtub and hung yard sale pictures over the holes in the paneling. Don was proud when she got pregnant. He charged a whole box of cigars at the B&M market and handed them out to his friends.

"You're supposed to do that when the baby is born, Don," Sally had told him. "What if they won't give us any more credit for groceries?" She had worn her arm in a sling for a week after that.

For months Sally had been making excuses. One day a fall. Another, a blind walk into a door or a chair or the table. She couldn't look Doc Parker in the eye during her exams. She prayed for Don to find the Lord. She prayed for patience. She prayed for forgiveness for whatever she did to deserve this. She prayed for strength.

If she weren't so tired from this pregnancy, from having Mikey glued to her all day, from sleeping with one eye open, perhaps she could figure out what to do.

She closed her eyes, and was startled awake by knocking. The front door opened. Mike slept on the bath mat next to the tub in a nest of toilet paper. The roll on the wall was empty.

"Yoo-hoo, Sally. You here?" It was Liza.

"I'm in the tub. Just a second." Her legs shook when she tried to stand, then her knees gave out. She slid back down into the tub, tossing water over the rim and onto the sleeping Mike. He woke with a howl. Liza barged on in.

"The door was unlocked." Liza stopped.

Sally saw her take in the whole scene—the baby in a mess of wet toilet paper, ink running on the note pinned to his back, her belly with its tell-tale marks, the black eye and split lip. Sally quit struggling. It wasn't her secret anymore.

"That bastard," Liza said. She scooped up Mike and stuck out a hand to Sally. "Let's get you dressed. You're coming with me."

∞

Sally lay on her side under stiff white sheets with blue stitching, tucked in so tightly her flaccid stomach beneath her hospital gown felt swollen and heavy as if she were still carrying the baby she had delivered four hours ago. Floating in a drug-induced womb of her own, she sensed the baby shift inside her and kick, but her hands found only folds of now-stretched skin over a belly stabbed by the phantoms that haunted all combat veterans who awoke missing parts. She heard the rustle of the nurse but took shallow breaths and feigned sleep.

She didn't want this private room. She wanted to be with the other mothers, lined up in the ward with cooing bundles at their breasts, or sticking toes into terrycloth mules and shuffling to the nursery window, stroking their husbands with the gentle finger-tips that brushed their babies' cheeks. She heard them murmuring, tapping on the glass. Her baby had clawed his way out of her body early, covered with a fine white hair. His broad stubby fingers and toes hadn't waited for nails before helping push his head into the light. Now he was paying for it, closed in a hot glass box and papoose-wrapped in cotton flannel.

Sally didn't know the doctor who delivered him, the man who held her son by the ankles for his first angry cry. She didn't know the man behind the mask who said, "This child is mongoloid," and left the room. Sally, her feet still in stirrups, had only a glimpse of her son's face, wide and flat-nosed, covered with fuzz, his eyes mere slits underneath beneath a broad forehead. From doctor to nurse to glass box, he was whisked from the room.

Sally's curtains caught a rare but welcome breeze this Fourth of July afternoon, and she turned toward it. Tears made the trek down her cheeks, stinging her split lip. She dabbed at them, then covered her face with her hands. She sobbed into her pillow for her still nameless boy child, for his now homeless brother, and for the cards she was dealt. Sally cried until she had nothing left.

It was Donnie's voice that woke her. She fumbled for her watch on the bed stand and the nurse call bell hit the floor and rolled. It was just after 7 o'clock, but morning or evening, she didn't know.

"They wouldn't tell me shit at the desk." She could hear Donnie in the hallway. "I got to hear it from some guy at the Standard station. I got a right to see him. I'm the God-damned father!" Sally heard something slap against glass.

"Your son was born early, Mr. Fisher. He's in an incubator." It was a nurse who answered.

"I can still see him, can't I?"

"Certainly, Mr. Fisher," the nurse's voice was calm. "I just have to wheel him up to the window."

Sally realized she'd been holding her breath. She wrapped her arms around her shoulders and took in air. Donnie was quiet, waiting. She imagined him standing there, pressing his face against the glass, shielding his eyes against the glare. He wasn't a bad man, just dealt some bad cards himself. He would be devastated.

"Hey," Donnie said. "What's wrong with him? He looks like a retard!"

His voice rose.

"You, get out here! What's wrong with him?"

"Mr. Fisher, why don't we sit down . . ." The nurse again.

"I'm not budging until I get some answers. This ain't my kid."

Fragments of the nurse's explanation filtered through the dark wood of Sally's door: Mongoloid . . . if he lives a year . . . institution. Just words for now.

"Where the hell's my wife?" Donnie interrupted.

Sally froze. Her sympathy dissolved in a rush of fear. She had expected him to be contrite. She touched her fingertips to her lips.

"I'm her God-damned husband. I got my rights!" Donnie didn't slur his words like some drunks. No, Sally knew he was drunk or he'd be charming the nurse instead of yelling. The nurse said something too low for Sally to hear, then the door slammed back against the wall inside her room. Donnie stood stock still, his hands on either side of the doorframe.

The nurse squeezed past him, picked the call bell off the floor and stood at the head of the bed. Donnie's nose was dark red. By tomorrow, Sally knew it would turn brown. He flashed even white teeth. Donnie leaned over the bed, and Sally could smell beer mixed with bourbon and the fishy mud of the White River. He spit words at her face.

"Running yesterday was the best thing you ever done. Saves me the trouble of kicking your ass out. My life turned to shit the day I married you. And that, that . . . thing in there's no more mine than that other brat a yours. There's no retards in my family, and there's never gonna be!"

"Mr. Fisher," the nurse stepped forward, but Donnie ignored her.

"You hear me?" Donnie yelled at Sally. He leaned over her, but Sally found the fear she felt moments ago was gone, replaced by the arctic stillness that crept through her after Winnan's death. She lay back on her pillows and stared at him. She saw his mouth moving, but there was no sound. She watched him like the horizon-wide screen at the drive-in movie, bigger than life, but as far away from the action as the bathroom behind the concession stand, his voice tinny and distorted like a metal speaker vibrating against the car window.

The nurse touched his elbow. Donnie shrugged her off. He stood, feet apart, braced to deliver or receive a blow, but there was no fight to be had. He took one last look at Sally and stomped out. Sally saw his reflection in the nursery glass, soft and fuzzy like the out-of-focus screen fade that every moviegoer knows cues the ending credits.

∞

It was just dark. Sally's food tray was intact save four soda crackers she'd washed down with milk. She could hear the pop of firecrackers, a precursor to the Jaycees' fireworks show along the river where Mike would be sitting on a blanket with Matt and Liza. She eased out of bed and wrapped up in her robe, the overlap now substantial without a belly full of child. The child she'd been unable to touch so far. Not able or not willing? Sally was no longer sure about anything. She looked up at the sky, trying to get her bearings, but it was too early for stars.

"You won't see fireworks out that one, Sally." It was Doc Parker.

Her throat got tight, and she couldn't speak. First deaf, now mute. She was falling apart. She stepped into the light and covered her black eye with her hand. Doc shook his head.

"What do you say we get some air?" He offered his arm. "I have reserved seats."

He steered her past the nurse's station, down a series of hallways onto a brick patio edged with a concrete ledge with uprights fat as September zucchini. A fragrant trellis of climbing roses stretched along one wall, the color of the blooms indistinct in the low light. Planter boxes held herbs Sally recognized—basil, rosemary, mint, sage. Beyond the patio low hills rolled toward the river.

Doc dusted off a chair with his handkerchief, and Sally lowered herself into its wide metal seat. Doc perched on the ledge.

There was a whistling like a rocket, then a pop, and the sky in front of them exploded into a waterfall of red. In the hollow space left behind was quiet clapping.

"I'm sorry I wasn't here for you," Doc said. "A tractor overturned and . . ."

"No matter," Sally said. "How could you know?"

A burst of green reflected off his glasses.

"And I should have gotten you out of there. When I first suspected."

Sally was silent. Would she have gone? Probably not.

They sat gazing at the horizon. The next few fireworks were singles, then a dud. The crowd below groaned.

"What are you going to name the boy?" Doc said.

Sally hadn't gotten that far. The names they picked out were all Fisher family names. Nothing like wrapping the child in yesterday's news. She shrugged.

"Did Dr. DeWitt talk to you? About the baby? About your options?"

Sally's throat swelled.

"He called him . . ." She coughed. "He called him a mongoloid. And then he just, just walked out."

She was crying now, tears running past her ears, down her neck. She rubbed at them with her hands, the collar of her robe. She moved to the edge of her chair, leaned toward Doc.

"Did I do something that hurt the baby? Did Don?"

"God, no, Sally. This isn't your fault. It just is. Being early, that could be from the trauma, but the other, it just is." Doc took her hand.

"There's all kinds of research on why, but what you've got in front of you is all that matters anyway. The way I see it, we've got two battles. The first one is that your little guy is premature. Did you take a good look at him?"

She shook her head.

"Well, he's got a lot of fine white hair. That's from being early. He doesn't have any fingernails or toenails, and his lungs aren't completely developed, but that doesn't keep him from crying. They'll come along as he gets stronger. His heart isn't as strong as I'd like it to be, but right now I can't tell if that's from being early or not. That's the first battle. Getting him through these first few weeks."

Sally sniffed. She had been so wrapped up in the other problems she hadn't realized how fragile the baby was.

"The second battle is that he's got the physical signs of mongoloid, and there's a lot we don't know about that. We do know for certain he will be retarded, but how much we won't know until he's older. He's going to be slow, slow at everything. Sitting up, crawling, walking, talking. His chances of making it past twelve are pretty slim. That's if he makes it through the first year. These kids have a lot of heart problems, like I said."

Sally couldn't imagine losing a child. Mikey? She shuddered. Losing Winnan was hard enough, but your own child.

"Prevailing practice is to recommend these kids be sent away—right away—before you get attached. There are places to get the care they need. A good one's up by Indianapolis. I can get the particulars if that's what you want to do."

"What would you do? If he were your child."

Doc wiped a hand across his face and turned toward the river as if gazing out to sea.

"No one ever said my opinion was worth a damn," Doc said, his voice gruff. "What does his father think?"

"He's out of the picture."

It was quiet on the patio. Sally heard crickets chirping.

"It must be time for the finale," she said. "There's always a break while they get it ready." She pushed against the arms of her chair as if to get up.

"You do know that none of this is your fault," Doc said.

"None of what? The baby? Or Don?"

"Both. And what happened to Winnan. All of it. It's not something you did or didn't do."

Sally wrapped her arms around her stomach and bowed her head.

"I know the Lord is testing me."

"I don't pretend to have the faith you do, Sally, but I do know you're stronger than you think."

"If I had been a better wife . . ."

"To who? Winnan or Don?"

"Either. But I was thinking of Winnan."

"Did Winnan confide in you, tell you his troubles?"

Sally shook her head.

"Then how could you help, Sally? He had a weakness, a sickness, that had nothing to do with you. There was nothing you could have done differently. Nothing."

Sally covered her face with her hands. Her shoulders shook.

"When I look at you I still see little Sally Sue Carson who wasn't going to take no for an answer once she fixed her mind on getting out of Dodge and going to college. That took some real courage. Whatever you think about her, I know she's still in there. A little bruised up maybe, but there."

"Do you believe God's doing this on purpose?"

"It doesn't matter what I believe. It only matters what you do. And what matters most right now is that you decide what you're going to do with that little boy in there. He's a gift. You can refuse him or embrace him, and no one will judge you except yourself."

The door opened behind them. A nurse called out a tentative, "Dr. Parker?"

"No rest for the weary," Sally said.

"Or the wicked," Doc said.

Another round of fireworks popped in the distance and with a whoosh and a whine the sky filled with rockets of primary colors, their sparks hanging in the sky like dandelion fluff or Spanish moss. Sally sat with her hands in her lap as they kept coming, whistling and pounding until finally a boom shook the ground and threw out a streaking ball of red, white, and blue in a celebration of independence.

Sally waited until a snake of headlights appeared in

the park, then stood on unsteady legs. She shuffled across the bricks and picked a rose from the trellis and held it to her nose. Inside the door she could see it was a pale pink, as soft as a baby's ear. Her baby's brand new ear. At the nursery she leaned against the railing underneath the picture window, looking for her son. He was nowhere in the two rows of newborns swaddled in pink or blue blankets.

She pushed on through the "Nurses Only" door, past the cradles on display and a lone brown rocking chair with no cushions. In an alcove away from the others, one baby lay fighting his blanket like a straightjacket, his mouth open wide. He screamed inside his glass enclosure. The sound was muffled, but the baby's face spoke more than the loudest scream. He was wet with tears, his skin red and blotched.

"There, there," Sally said. She pressed her fingertips against the smooth surface. He kept on screaming.

"You can't be back here."

A masked nurse Sally didn't recognize was washing her hands.

"You're not supposed to be here. This one is in isolation."

"Is he contagious?"

"He's premature. We keep him warm and isolated for his own good." The nurse dried her hands on a towel fresh from an autoclave. "Do you need help back to your room?"

Sally looked at the boy.

"He's crying." He barely stopped to get a breath. His face was getting redder.

"I can see that. It won't hurt him. He'll learn that crying won't do him any good, and he'll quit. Better for him in the long run. They all learn that eventually."

"All premature babies?" Sally's hands caressed the glass.

"All the retarded ones. If you don't leave I'll have to get the doctor."

Sally took a deep breath and pulled her shoulders back.

"You do that."

The nurse turned on a white rubber heel and disappeared through a wall of stainless steel machines at the back of the alcove. Sally washed her hands and opened the sterilizer for a clean towel. She spread the towel across her chest. The incubator was easier to open than she thought. The crying was deafening now, the baby's anger and desperation unleashed, as painful as if he were still inside her, kicking and clawing.

"There, there, little one," Sally cooed, scooping her son into her arms. "It's going to be all right."

She rotated the chair with her foot to face the other babies and nestled her tiny boy in the warm space between her breasts. She inhaled his baby smell and kissed the down on the top of his head. He quieted immediately, and Sally hoped it was because he recognized her, lulled by the familiar rhythm of her heart. Did he know it was his mother who had come to rescue him, or would he bond with just anyone, so hungry for comfort, for touch? He wasn't going to have much of a life going from glass cage to institution, now was he?

Sally sang a song of the paw paw patch and rocked her son to sleep. Through the glass she could see the tattle-tale nurse with her mask hanging off one ear, dragging Doc Parker toward the nursery. She pointed at Sally, even more animated once she saw the baby on her chest. Doc Parker looked at Sally through the glass and grinned.

Book Club Discussion Ideas

1. Who chose the book and why?

2. Many of the stories are set in the south—how do the stories fulfill or transcend Southern literature as a genre?

3. Heuring's stories use a wide range of narrators, from an adolescent in "Chaperone for Cousin Katie," a senior citizen in "One Chair Away," a college boy in "Roommates," to a domestic abuse victim in "What Liza Saw." Which character(s) most appealed to you and why?

4. Nearly all of the stories deal with loss. How do the different characters deal with their loss? Are some more equipped than others to make it through the stages of grief?

5. There are bizarre plot points in several stories: a woman is trapped by a pie safe, a man blows himself up, a man is killed by a shoe. How does humor in a tragic circumstance affect how you view the story?

6. In the story "What Liza Saw," Sally saw the consequences of her choices played out in her marriage to Donnie. What were her decision points to make changes? Do you think she made the right choices in the end? Use the issues in these questions as a starting point for other stories in the collection.

7. Would your mother do this? Pick any of the women in this collection and put your mother in her place. What would your mother do?